Poker Face

"Just keep your hand in the bag, friend," Eddie said.

Clint looked at Eddie and the double-barreled Greener he was holding.

"I'm not surprised," he said.

"You're not?" Eddie asked. "Good for you. Cesar, get his gun."

"Forget it, Cesar," Clint said. "It's not in my holster."

"It's not?" Eddie asked. "Where is it?"

"It's in my hand, in this bag," Clint said.

Eddie grinned. "You're bluffing. Cesar, get his gun, and his money."

"If Cesar comes near me, I'll pull the trigger," Clint said. "If you don't put that shotgun down, I'll pull the trigger."

"Go ahead, Cesar," Eddie said. "He's bluffin'."

Cesar walked tentatively toward Clint, and when he came within view of the holster, he saw that it was empty.

"Aw, Eddie—" he said.

Clint cut him off by pulling the trigger of his concealed Colt. The bullet tore through the bottom of the bag and drilled Eddie right through the chest. Clint hit the floor and upended the table. Eddie pulled both triggers of his shotgun as he died.

The shotgun made a hellacious noise. The shot spread out and struck the table and the wall behind Clint.

Then it was quiet.

THE GUNSMITH

391

SHOWDOWN IN DESPERATION

J. R. ROBERTS

JOVE BOOKS, NEW YORK

THE BERKLEY PUBLISHING GROUP
Published by the Penguin Group
Penguin Group (USA) LLC
375 Hudson Street, New York, New York 10014

USA • Canada • UK • Ireland • Australia • New Zealand • India • South Africa • China

penguin.com

A Penguin Random House Company

SHOWDOWN IN DESPERATION

A Jove Book / published by arrangement with the author

For information, address: The Berkley Publishing Group,
a division of Penguin Group (USA) LLC,
375 Hudson Street, New York, New York 10014.

ISBN: 978-0-515-15482-5

PUBLISHING HISTORY
Jove mass-market edition / July 2014

PRINTED IN THE UNITED STATES OF AMERICA

10 9 8 7 6 5 4 3 2

Cover illustration by Sergio Giovine.

ONE

The stopover in El Legado, New Mexico, was supposed to be a leisurely one. A few drinks, a few women, some poker. Easy. Lay low. Stay out of trouble. More and more difficult these days, for some reason, but Clint Adams was determined to try really hard this time.

So then why was he out here, no provisions, on the hunt, and yet on the run at the same time?

It had all started out so well . . .

Settling in was easy. It was all a routine. Find a livery for Eclipse, make sure the hostler knows what he's doing and will properly care for the Darley Arabian, and get himself settled in a decent hotel. Then leave his saddlebags and rifle in the room and go out to find something to eat.

He found a café the first day that was doing a good business. It either had good food, or it was the only place in town. He went in, got himself a table, discovered—with a steak and vegetables—that it had decent food. The coffee was strong and good, too.

He paid his bill and walked the town, impressed that it was larger than he had first thought. There were several hotels and salons, more restaurants and cafés. The smell of fresh-cut wood in the air spoke to the fact that new buildings were being built.

Of the several saloons he passed, he chose the largest, which was called The Wagon Wheel. Inside he saw a huge wagon wheel hanging over the back of the bar where most saloons had paintings of naked women. All things being equal, he preferred the paintings—but this was obviously cheaper for the owner.

He had a beer, looked over the operation, and then went back to his hotel. It wasn't until the next day that he went back and took a seat at what looked to be an ongoing poker game.

And he started to win.

That should have been a good thing . . .

He checked his back trail, didn't see any indication that the posse had gotten closer.

He turned his attention to the trail he was following. It was still fresh, but there continued to be no sign of a rider ahead of him.

It was difficult to track and hunt someone when you yourself were being hunted.

He'd never been in this situation before. He shook his head. How the hell . . .

He played poker for a few days, found one of the saloon girls to his liking. Her name was Jenny. She was in her thirties, a strawberry blonde with large breasts and a majestic butt. In bed she was voracious, and he particularly liked how bountiful her blond pubic bush was.

On the fourth night they were engaged in a particularly energetic romp in his room when they both rolled off the bed onto the floor. Lucky for Jenny, Clint was on the bottom.

"Ouch!" she said.

"Hey," he said, "I cushioned your fall."

"I hit my elbow."

"I landed on my rump."

She wriggled atop him, felt his cock still rock hard inside her.

"It doesn't seem to have affected your performance."

"It would take a lot more than a fall out of bed to do that," he said, reaching around to cup her buttocks. "Do you want to get back in bed?"

She sat up on him, wriggled again, and thought.

"No," she said, "I . . . I don't think you've been this deep before."

"It's the floor," he said. "No give."

"Mmm," she said, rising up and then coming down on him. "Oh!"

"Go ahead," he said. "You won't hurt me."

She started bouncing up and down on him, groaning and grunting each time she came down. Her big breasts began to bounce and bob in front of him, the pink nipples swollen with passion. He tried to catch them with his mouth and succeeded about half the time.

"Oh yes," she said, "this is nice . . . this is very nice . . ."

She slowed down so she could truly enjoy the way it felt to have him that deep. At one point she stopped bouncing and began to grind herself down on him.

"Oh God," she said, "is—is that all right for you?"

"It's fine for me," he breathed. "Keep going."

She pressed her hands down on his chest, began to rotate her hips while still grinding.

"Wow," she said, "wow . . . I've never . . . done it like this . . . before."

"Never had sex on the floor before?"

"No," she gasped, "usually . . . in a bed."

"It's always good," he grunted, "to try something . . . new."

"Mmm," she said, biting her lip and closing her eyes. He felt her tremble, her legs, her thighs, then saw her belly spasm—and suddenly she was riding him like a bucking bronco, gasping and crying out.

And then he exploded.

TWO

Clint remembered that time with Jenny fondly, now that he was on horseback and being pursued. He looked up at the sun. He hadn't had time to pack supplies, and his canteen was only half full. Playing poker was supposed to have been relaxing, and for a while it was . . .

The game was five-card stud, with six players. The stakes were not high, but Clint was making beer and food money since he sat down.

The other five players had varying degrees of skill.

Dan Brennan was a local store owner who seemed to spend an inordinate time away from his store. In his fifties, he played adequately, but with no great skill.

Hank Wilkins was a drifter in his thirties who had arrived just a couple of days ahead of Clint. He didn't know the other players any better than Clint did.

Other than Clint, the only other player doing any winning was Carl Lanigan. He was a gambler who had drifted into town looking for a game. Finding this one, he had busted several regulars out of the game already, making room for both Wilkins and Clint. But when Clint sat down, the fortyish gambler started winning less.

The two big losers were Hugo Dargo, about fifty-five, who had been living in town for many years, though no one seemed to know where he had come from. He owned a hardware store and, like Brennan, seemed to spend more time at the poker table than in his store. He never lost his good humor even while he was losing his money.

The bad loser at the table was Johnny Creed. He was in his late twenties, arrogant without reason. He fancied himself good with cards, and good with a gun, but he was a bad loser, and a bad player. Clint had no idea how good he was with his handgun. He didn't intend to find out.

Clint sat at the table on the fifth day and said, "Deal me in."

"We almost gave away your seat," Dargo said. "Thought you wasn't comin' back."

"Just a little late getting started today," Clint said. Jenny had kept him in bed longer than usual. Or rather, on the floor.

"Well, you're just in time to deal," Brennan said, passing the deck to him.

Clint shuffled, allowed Lanigan to cut, and said, "Comin' out."

About midday the sheriff walked in, went to the bar for his afternoon beer. His name was Matthews, he was in his fifties, and he didn't seem at all concerned that the Gunsmith was in his town. He usually came in and had one beer, just one, without paying—but Clint wondered if he did the same thing in every saloon in town.

"Afternoon, Sheriff," Brennan called.

"Dan," the lawman said, raising his beer. "How you doin' today?"

"Still losing to Mr. Adams here," Brennan said.

"So am I," Dargo said.

"We all are," Lanigan, the gambler, said.

"Well, I ain't," Creed said, "not with this hand. I bet five dollars."

"That's a big bet for this game," Brennan pointed out.

"Then fold," Creed said. "I'm tryin' to get my money back."

"I don't object," Lanigan said. "I call the five."

Clint looked down at his cards, one down and two up, two to come. Creed was showing two eights. He either had a third one in the hole, or he wanted them to think so.

"Call," Clint said.

Brennan did, indeed, fold, as did Dargo and Wilkins.

Brennan, who was dealing, said, "Pot's right. Cards comin' out."

He dealt a fourth card to Lanigan, Clint, and Creed. The sheriff watched from the bar with interest, nursing his beer.

Lanigan received a nine to go along with a five and a six of different suits.

Clint had a ten, a jack, and now a king in front of him, all mismatched suits.

Creed watched a jack fall on his two eights. Absolutely no help, unless his hole card was actually a jack.

"Ha!" he said.

"Your bet, Johnny," Brennan said, setting the deck down on the table.

"Yeah, yeah," the youngest man at the table said. "How about ten dollars?"

"Like I said when you bet five—" Brennan started, but Lanigan stopped him.

"It's okay, Brennan," Lanigan said. "I'll call his bet, and raise his ten."

"What?" Creed asked.

Lanigan smiled.

"I'll call the bet and the raise," Clint said.

Creed looked unnerved, but then firmed his chin and said, "I raise twenty."

A couple of the players raised their eyebrows. The play went to Lanigan.

"Well, well," he said, "you must have a pretty good hand, young man."

"It's okay," Creed said. "Worth another twenty anyway."

"Yeah, well," Lanigan said, "I'll just call the twenty, since we all have another card coming."

"Adams?" Brennan asked. "In or out?"

"Oh, I'm in," Clint said, tossing the twenty into the pot.

"Okay," Brennan said, picking up the deck, "pot's right."

He dealt each man his fifth and last card.

Lanigan got an eight to go with his five, six, and nine.

Clint received a nine to go with his ten, jack, and king.

"Possible straight, possible straight," Brennan said, then dealt Creed a second jack. "And two pair. Possible full house."

He placed the deck down on the table.

"Your bet, son," he said to Creed.

"Don't call me son," the younger man said.

"Sorry," Brennan said. "Your bet, Mr. Creed."

Creed looked at the money in front of him. They were playing with chips, and he had a small stack left.

"Fifty dollars," he said. "That's all I got left."

"I could raise," Lanigan said.

"I told you," Creed said, "I have no more money."

"If he raises," Brennan pointed out, "and you can't call, he takes the pot."

"Or I do," Clint reminded him.

"That's right," Lanigan said.

"You goddamn—" Creed started, but Lanigan cut him off.

"But I won't," he said. "I'll just call you, boy."

"Don't call me—"

"I'll call the bet, too," Clint said, "much as I'd like to raise."

Lanigan looked at him.

"You'd like to raise?"

"I would."

"Well," Lanigan said, "would you be interested in, say, a side pot?"

"A side pot?"

"Yeah," Lanigan said, "one just between you and me."

"You can't do that!" Creed said.

"It's up to them, son," Brennan said. "You're out of it."

"Don't call me son."

"Just keep quiet," Brennan said. "We all want to see how this plays out."

"Whataya say?" Lanigan asked.

"Whose bet is it?"

"Yours," the gambler said. "You said you wanted to raise. So raise."

THREE

"Fifty," Clint said.

"Dollars?" Creed blurted out.

"Shhh," Brennan said.

"Nice bet," Lanigan said.

"It's your play, Mr. Lanigan," Brennan said. As the dealer, even though he was out of the hand, he was still the general at the table.

"Your fifty," Lanigan said, "and a hundred more."

"Your play, Mr. Adams," Brennan said.

Creed looked at the pot in the center of the table—the one he was still part of. Then he looked at the side pot, which dwarfed his.

"I'll call your hundred," Clint said.

"That's all?" Lanigan asked.

"Why not?" Clint said. "There are other hands to be played. Right?"

"You're right," Lanigan said.

"And you're called," Clint said.

"Pot's right," Brennan said. "Whataya got, kid?"

Creed, as if he already knew he was beat, turned up his hole card.

"Three eights."

"Mr. Lanigan?"

The gambler turned up his card.

"Straight to the nine."

"You're beat, kid," Brennan said. "Mr. Adams?"

Clint turned his card over.

"Straight to the ace," he said.

"Mr. Adams wins both pots."

"Well played," Lanigan said to Clint.

Clint raked his pots in.

"The deal's yours," Brennan said to Lanigan.

The gambler gathered the cards and shuffled them.

"You still in, kid?" he asked.

"Naw," Creed said, "I'm busted."

"Too bad," Lanigan said. He tossed a chip across the table. "Have a drink on me."

"Sure," Creed said. He picked up the chip and left the table. Another body filled it.

"Table stakes," Lanigan said to him.

"Sounds good," the man said.

"Comin' out," Lanigan said, and dealt.

Johnny Creed went to the bar for his drink, gave the bartender the chip.

"Whataya have?" the barman asked.

"Whiskey."

"Tough beat," the bartender said, pouring the kid his drink.

Creed downed his drink and said, "They cheated me."

"You think so?"

"I know so," Creed said, "and I'm gonna get even."

"How you gonna do that?"

"I don't know yet," Creed said. "But I'll figure it out."

The sheriff, who had finished up his beer, leaned over and said, "Don't go lookin' for trouble, son."

As the lawman laughed, Creed seethed, "Don't call me son!"

"That boy's a real bad loser," Brennan said, back at the poker table.

"Is that supposed to be a warning?" Clint asked while Lanigan shuffled.

"I'm just sayin', is all," Brennan said with a shrug. "He don't like to lose."

"Then he shouldn't play," Lanigan said, "because he's always going to lose."

"He's pretty slick with that gun, too," Wilkins said, adding his two cents.

"Are you telling me, or him?" Lanigan said, jerking his head toward Clint.

"It don't matter," Wilkins said. "Like Brennan, I'm just sayin'."

"Well, then, deal the cards, Mr. Lanigan," Clint said. "I can't start worrying about bad losers who may or may not be good with a gun."

"Comin' out," Lanigan said, dealing the first card. "Ah, big ace for the Gunsmith. It's your bet, my friend . . ."

FOUR

Clint reined Eclipse in and stroked the big gelding's neck. There was no sign of anyone in front of him, or behind him, and it was starting to get dark. It seemed safe to camp now.

He found a likely clearing, unsaddled Eclipse, rubbed him down, and allowed him to graze. After that he built a fire. He had no coffee, but he did have some beef jerky in his saddlebag. He sat in front of the fire, munched on the dried meat, sipped his water while hoping to find a water-hole the next morning. Or a town—a small town, without a telegraph office, where they would not have yet heard about what had happened in El Legado.

If he was going to keep hunting—and running—he was going to need some supplies.

He stared out into the darkness, thought back to his time in the New Mexican town . . .

After Clint took the big pot from Lanigan, the game settled back to normal, with five- and ten-dollar bets. Clint and the gambler continued to win, and before long the newcomer who had taken Johnny Creed's seat busted out. From that point on, they played five-handed, until the bartender came over and said, "Gotta close up, gents."

"Back here tomorrow?" Brennan asked.

"Suits me," Lanigan said.

Everyone agreed.

"Buy you a beer?" Lanigan asked Clint.

"If the bartender will sell it."

"He will," Lanigan said with a smile. "I got pull."

While the others left, they walked to the bar and Lanigan called out, "Jasper, one more beer for me and my friend."

"Comin' up," Jasper said, "but then you fellas gotta go."

"Of course."

The barman, who, at fifty, was the owner of his first saloon after tending bar for twenty-five years in other people's, served them a beer each.

This was actually Clint's first ever since early in the evening. He never drank when he was playing.

As for Henry Lanigan, he'd been drinking beer all night, but seemed no worse for the wear.

"You play poker very well," Lanigan said. "Learned from good players?"

"The best," Clint said. "I've sat at a lot of tables with Bat Masterson and Luke Short."

Lanigan's eyebrows went up.

"That is the best. Wish I had some time against players like that myself."

"There's still plenty of time," Clint said. "How often have you played in Denver, or San Francisco?"

"I haven't played there yet," Lanigan said. "But I intend to. Soon."

"I'm sure you'll fit in just fine."

"Think so?"

"You play well enough."

"Thanks."

"How long do you plan to stay in town?" Clint asked.

"Just a few more days," Lanigan said. "I've almost won enough of a stash, although it's hard to put it together with such low stakes. Oh, and you did take a chunk of it away from me with that side pot."

"Sorry about that."

"Oh, that's okay," Lanigan said. "After all, it was my idea. I tried to take advantage of the situation and gouge you."

"That poor kid got caught in the middle," Clint said.

"Yes, he did," Lanigan said, "and he didn't like it. He's liable to come after one, or both of us."

"That would be his problem."

"Well," Lanigan said, "we better just watch our backs." He put his empty mug down.

"Thanks for the beer, Lanigan," Clint said, setting his mug down as well. "Where are you staying?"

"A rooming house in town," Lanigan said as they walked to the door. "I didn't have much money when I got here. I've actually been having a streak of bad luck."

"Seems to have improved."

"A bit," Lanigan said. "I was doing better before you came along."

"Again," Clint said, "sorry."

"No need to apologize," Lanigan said. "I like a spirited game." They stepped outside and Jasper locked the door behind them.

"What about you?" Lanigan asked. "How much longer do you intend to hang around?"

"Only a day or two," Clint said. "I could stay out of the game, if you like."

"No need."

"But I was just passing the time," Clint said. "You need the stake."

"I'll get my stake." Lanigan pointed. "My rooming house is this way."

Clint pointed the other way.

"My hotel's that way."

"Then I'll see you tomorrow," Lanigan said. "Remember. Watch your back."

"You, too."

They separated and went their own ways.

When Clint entered his room, he found Jenny on the bed.

"I didn't see you at work tonight," he said.

"How could you?" she asked from the bed. "You were concentrating so hard."

"That's how you win."

She tossed the sheet back to reveal herself to be completely naked beneath it.

"Why don't you try concentrating that hard on me?" she asked.

He smiled and said, "That's just what I was thinking."

FIVE

Clint sat in front of the fire, kept his eyes away from the flames, kept his ears open while bringing back the memory of Jenny in his bed . . .

Her body was smooth and full, so full that sometimes he felt as if she would burst when he bit into her breasts and cover him with sweet juice, like a ripe piece of fruit. But not fat, never fat.

When he had her on her hands and knees and was fucking her from behind, there seemed to be acres of glorious flesh in front of him. He ran his hands over the muscles of her back, smacked her on the butt until her cheeks were red, and then gripped her by the hips to steady her as he plunged into her. And then he'd roar—actually roar, like a lion or a bull—when he ejaculated inside her . . .

* * *

He shook his head to dispel the image, because he felt himself swelling, and that was like being all dressed up with no place to go.

He stoked his fire, ate his last piece of beef jerky, and drank the last of his water. He had nothing left for breakfast, so in the morning he'd have to rise, saddle up, and ride immediately, hoping to find either a water hole or a small town.

The best thing now was to roll himself up in his bedroll and get some sleep. If anyone approached during the night, he knew that he'd hear from Eclipse . . .

Back in El Legado he woke the next morning, rolled over, and bumped into Jenny, who didn't stir. She was fast asleep, exhausted from their night together. He could feel their exertions in his legs, but his manifested itself not in exhaustion, but hunger.

He dressed quietly and slipped from the room, even though he thought he could fire his gun without waking her. In the lobby he made a quick decision, decided to go back to the café he'd eaten at on his first day and have breakfast there.

He stepped outside onto the busy main street, ducking a rider and an oncoming buckboard as he crossed over. On the other side he ran into the sheriff, who was just standing there with his hands on his guns—he wore two—watching the street.

Sheriff Tom Cox was a dandy. In his fifties, he had gray hair, a well-cared-for gray mustache, and a bit of a potbelly that maybe he thought wearing two guns could hide.

"Mornin', Adams," he said.

"Sheriff," Clint said, joining the man on the boardwalk. "You sure do have a busy town here."

"Indeed we do," the sheriff said. "We're growin' by leaps and bounds. Got a new church and a new school."

Clint had also heard talk of the town council bringing in a new police station, which would mean the sheriff's job would be reduced, or eliminated. He didn't mention that, though.

"Quite a game last night," Cox said.

"Small stakes," Clint said.

"For you, maybe," Cox said, "not for the folks in this town. Not for Johnny Creed."

"He shouldn't play if he can't lose gracefully," Clint said.

"And every professional gambler you know is a graceful loser?" Cox asked.

"No," Clint said, "but they're professional. He's not. He's liable to lose his temper and cause a lot of trouble."

"With his gun, you mean."

"I've heard stories . . ."

"Well, he does fancy himself a fast gun," Cox said, "and I've heard that he's pretty accurate."

"Has he ever killed a man?"

"Not that I know of."

"Well, he'll find that a lot more difficult than target shooting," Clint said. "I'm off to have some breakfast."

"Enjoy it," Cox said. "I'll see you at the saloon later in the day when I stop in for my beer. I'm sure you'll be deep into your game by then."

"I'm sure I will," Clint said. "Have a good day."

The sheriff tipped his hat to some passing ladies then said to Clint, "You, too."

Clint walked to the café, found it doing a brisk morning business, but was able to get a table against the wall. Most people liked to sit where they could look out the window. Not him.

He was deep into his steak and eggs when Dan Brennan walked in. At that time there were no tables so Clint waved, got his attention, and beckoned him over.

"Join me," he invited.

"Thanks."

The waiter came over and Brennan pointed at Clint's plate, pouring himself a cup of coffee.

"So, figure on stayin' in town much longer?" the storekeeper asked.

"Not too much longer," Clint said. "But I'll play a day or two more."

"What do you think of our little game?"

"It's a way to pass the time."

"That's how most of us feel," Brennan said. "But not the gambler, Lanigan. He's tryin' to build a stake."

"Hard way to do it."

"He's gettin' there, little by little."

"And then there's Creed," Clint said.

"Yes," Brennan said, "he's kind of intense."

"He shouldn't be playing poker," Clint said. "Not with men anyway."

"We all know that," Brennan said, "but we're still willing to take his money."

"He's not a good loser," Clint said. "It's dangerous to let him play."

Brennan grinned and said, "He ain't mad at me. Maybe you and Lanigan."

"We'll watch our backs," Clint said.

"Oh, I don't know that the boy is a backshooter," Brennan said. "Now his old man , . ."

"Who's his father?"

"Oh, you didn't know?" Brennan asked. "Jimmy Creed is his dad."

Clint had heard of Jimmy Creed. The man was a notorious backshooter. Clint thought Johnny Creed was probably just trying to make people think he was Jimmy. He didn't expect that the boy was related.

"Creed was from here?" Clint asked.

"Married a girl from here years ago," Brennan said, "stayed around long enough for her to get pregnant, then moved on and continued to make his reputation."

"Shooting men in the back isn't much of a reputation," Clint said.

Brennan shrugged, sat back so the waiter could put his breakfast on the table.

"Thanks," he said, and dug in.

Clint was concerned. If Jimmy Creed fancied himself to be his father's son, what was to keep him from trying to shoot Clint or Lanigan in the back?

He needed to make sure Lanigan was aware.

SIX

After breakfast Clint went in search of Lanigan's rooming house. The man hadn't said where it was, except to point in a direction. He walked toward that end of town, keeping his eyes open. He came to the end of what seemed to be the town limits. There were no more storefronts, just a few residential houses. One of them was two stories and certainly looked large enough to be a rooming house.

He approached it, stepped to the door, and knocked. A handsome woman answered the door, stood there drying her hands on her apron. Her auburn hair was pinned up over her head, a few tendrils escaping and flopping down over her forehead.

"Yes?"

"I'm sorry to bother you," Clint said, "but . . . is this a rooming house?"

"It is, indeed," the woman said, with what seemed to be a slight Irish accent, "but I'm afraid I have no rooms available at the moment."

"That's all right," he said, "I'm not looking for a room, I'm looking for a man I think may be one of your roomers."

She finished drying her hands and perched them on her hips.

"Oh? And who might that be?"

"His name is Carl Lanigan."

"Ah, yes, Mr. Lanigan has a room here," she said. "Would you be wantin' to talk to him?" The Irish lilt suddenly became more pronounced.

"I would," he said.

"Come in, then."

"Thank you."

He stepped inside and followed her to a large living room area.

"My boarders have had their breakfast, but I believe I have some coffee left. Would you like a cup?"

"Yes, thank you."

"I'll tell Mr. Lanigan you're here," she said. "I believe he sleeps late and works later in the day."

"I believe he does," Clint agreed.

"Please, have a seat."

The furniture was functional, not fancy. A woman didn't usually turn her home into a rooming house unless she needed the money. In most case, they were widows.

She returned with a tray bearing a pot of coffee and two cups.

"You gentlemen can have coffee in here and talk," she said. "He'll be coming down those stairs any min—ah, here he is."

Lanigan came down the stairs in shirtsleeves, the first

time Clint had seen him when he wasn't wearing his gambler's suit.

"Well, good morning," he said. "When Mrs. O'Shea told me there was a man here to see me, I was afraid it was that young pup."

"And you came down without a gun?"

Lanigan took a small derringer from his trouser pocket.

"Gentlemen," Mrs. O'Shea said, "I want no gunplay in my house."

"Don't worry, Erin," Lanigan said, putting the derringer back in his pocket, "this is my friend Clint Adams. Clint, meet my landlady, Erin O'Shea."

"Miss O'Shea."

"Mrs.," she said. "I'm a widow. It's a pleasure to meet you. I'll leave you to it now."

She turned and went into the kitchen.

Lanigan sat across from Clint. They poured coffee and then sat back.

"What brings you here?"

"Actually, it is that young pup, Creed," Clint said.

"What about him?" Lanigan asked. "He didn't make a try for you last night, did he?"

"No, but I found out that his father is Jimmy Creed."

"Jimmy Creed," Lanigan said, frowning and shaking his head. "I don't know—"

"Jimmy Creed is a notorious backshooter," Clint said. "Johnny is his son."

"Oh," Lanigan said, "I see. You're thinkin' like father, like son?"

"As far as I know," Clint said, "the kid has never killed anyone . . . yet."

"Always a first time," the gambler said. "So you came to warn me?"

"Yes."

Lanigan raised his cup.

"You have my thanks. I'll watch my back—but I was going to do that anyway."

Clint sipped the coffee—which was weak—and set his cup down.

"Tell Mrs. O'Shea I said thanks for the coffee."

"Terrible stuff, isn't it?"

Clint smiled. Both men stood up.

"Worth it, though. She's quite a handsome woman."

"Are you more than just a boarder, then?"

"No," Lanigan said, "not yet anyway."

The gambler walked Clint to the front door.

"I'll see you tonight at the game," he said as Clint went out the door.

"Yep," Clint said, "see you there."

He went down the steps while the gambler closed the door behind him.

Now that they were both forewarned, he felt a little better about Johnny Creed. They'd have to be very careless to end up getting shot in the back.

The Gunsmith was never careless.

Lanigan went back inside, found Mrs. O'Shea waiting there, holding the tray.

"Trouble?" she asked.

"No, dear lady," he said, "nothing to worry about."

"Will you be going out earlier, then?"

"No," he said, "just the usual time."

"So you'll be having supper here?"

"Yes, ma'am," he said. "Why would I go anywhere else when I can have your fine Irish cooking?"

She smiled broadly and said, "Beef stew tonight."

A lovely lass, he thought as she went into the kitchen, but her cooking did leave something to be desired.

SEVEN

When Clint entered the saloon, the game was already in play. Brennan and the other locals had started without him and Carl Lanigan.

"Gentlemen," Clint said, stopping at the table.

"Pull up your chair, Adams," Brennan said.

"I'll be right over," Clint said, "I just need to have a beer first."

"Oh, that's right," Dargo said. "You don't drink while you play."

"Maybe we'd better try to get him drunk, huh?" Brennan asked, and they all laughed.

Clint walked to the bar and ordered a beer from Jasper, the bartender. As he was drinking it, Lanigan walked in, saw him, and smiled. He was in full gear—black suit, flowered silk vest, and a boiled white short. He walked directly to the table and sat down, but he waved at Jasper, who sent over a beer for him with one of the girls.

As Clint was finishing his beer, Jenny appeared, came over to the bar to check in with Jasper.

"You ready to work finally?" Jasper asked.

"I needed my beauty sleep," she told him, "but I'm ready."

"You know," the bartender said, handing her a tray, "I have younger women who want your job."

"A younger woman couldn't do my job as well, Jasper," she said. "Don't threaten me, or I might take you up on it."

She turned, gave Clint a wink, and waded into the throng to start working.

Clint finished his beer and set the mug down on the bar.

"Is she right?" he asked Jasper.

"Unfortunately," Jasper said. "I'd like to fire her, but I don't dare."

Clint nodded, walked over to the poker table, and pulled out his chair . . .

As he awoke in camp, he remembered how he'd felt that day in the saloon. He was . . . uncomfortable, and there was no apparent reason for it.

He looked around as he sat, saw nothing that would cause him any concern. In fact, everything was fine the first hour he was there, and he was just starting to relax when Johnny Creed came through the batwings . . .

"Don't look now," Brennan said, "but Johnny just came in."

"I see him," Clint said.

"He's not gonna play tonight," Dargo said.

"He can if he wants—" Lanigan started, but Dargo cut him off.

"No," Dargo said, "after we left last night and you and Adams stayed to have a drink, the rest of us voted to keep him out of the game."

"That's fine with me," Clint said.

"He might have some fresh money," Lanigan said.

"We don't care," Brennan said.

"Well, okay," Lanigan said with a shrug. "It's your game."

But Johnny Creed didn't try to get into the game—at least, not right away. He remained at the bar, drinking beers as fast as Jasper could pour them. Clint was sitting where he could see the bar, and he knew that trouble was coming.

Lanigan started out hot, winning the first three hands he played, two with the best cards, and one when he bluffed out both Brennan and Wilkins.

Clint was sitting with two kings on the table and one in the hole when Johnny Creed decided to come on over.

"I'm sittin' in," he said, reaching for the one empty chair.

"No, you ain't," Dargo said, kicking the chair back in.

"What?"

"You can't play, Johnny," Brennan said. "Not in this game."

"I got money!"

"We don't care," Wilkins said. "You're out."

Creed glared at all the men at the table.

"Don't look at me like that," Lanigan said. "I got out-voted."

The boy looked at Clint.

"Hey," he said with a shrug, "it's their game."

Creed fumed, then said, "Well, ain't nobody can stop me from watchin'!"

"Not so long as you watch from over there," Brennan said, indicating the bar.

"You'll be sorry," he said, and stomped over to the bar to have another beer.

"Whose bet?" Brennan asked.

"Mine," Clint said. "I'll bet two dollars."

EIGHT

Clint took that hand with the three kings, and then they started going back Lanigan's way again. Still, Clint was well ahead for the past few days that he had been playing.

Creed remained at the bar, drinking. At one point he began to complain loudly to anyone who would listen, and to everyone who wouldn't.

The game was quiet for a couple of hours, hands going around the table, being won and lost by everyone. No one had taken charge for a while, and then a hand began to develop.

Wilkins was dealing. Lanigan had two jacks on the table, Clint two tens. Brennan had three hearts. Dargo had already folded. Wilkins himself had a pair of threes he was trying to ride to the end.

Brennan said, "I bet ten."

"Okay," Lanigan said, "this has been boring long enough. I raise twenty."

"I also raise twenty," Clint said without hesitation.

"I'll call both raises," Wilkins said. "Your play, Brennan."

"I'll call," Brennan said. "A lot can happen with the last cards."

"Pot's right. Comin' out," Wilkins said.

He dealt everyone their fourth card. Lanigan and Clint received no discernible help. The same for Wilkins, but Brennan had a fourth heart fall on the table. His face betrayed nothing.

"Well," Wilkins said, "isn't this interesting." He set the deck down. "Brennan?"

Brennan hesitated just long enough for Clint to figure that he was nervous. He was about to make a bet he wasn't sure he could afford.

"Bet fifty."

"Ah," Lanigan said, "now it gets interesting."

"What do you do, Lanigan?" Wilkins asked.

"I call the fifty," Lanigan said, "and raise fifty more."

"Adams?" Wilkins said.

"Hmm," Clint said, "you fellas really like your hands. I guess I'll call the bet and the raise . . . and I raise a hundred."

Wilkins looked at his hole card and shook his head.

"I can't believe this," he said, "but I'm gonna fold."

He turned his cards facedown on the table. Clint was sure the man had three threes.

"Brennan?" Wilkins said. "Bet your possible flush."

"Interesting," Brennan said. He stared at Lanigan, then at Clint, and finally shook his head and turned his cards down. He was bluffing and could not keep it going.

"That leaves the two of you," Wilkins said.

"A hundred," Lanigan said.

"Big pot," Clint said. He wondered if he should make it bigger. He had three tens, and he was almost certain Lanigan had three jacks. He'd be a fool to raise. The gambler was not about to be bluffed. Not with three jacks.

"I'll call."

Lanigan turned over his hole card. A jack.

Clint laughed, showed his third ten.

"Good hand, Lanigan."

"I folded three threes," Wilkins said.

"Good fold," Clint said.

Lanigan raked in his chips while Brennan collected the cards. Lanigan had taken back part of what Clint had taken off him.

"Oh, hey!" Creed yelled. "The famous gunman was taken to school in that one! How does it feel, Gunsmith? Bein' the big loser?"

Clint rolled his eyes and ignored the young man's jibes. Creed eventually fell silent, and the game continued . . .

Later, as the saloon began to empty out, Wilkins, and then Dargo, called it a night. That left Brennan, Lanigan, and Clint. Brennan had actually started to win late in the day. However, the pots he took usually came at the expense of his fellow townsmen.

"Gettin' late," Brennan said. "Jasper's gonna kick us out soon—again."

Clint looked at the bar. Even Creed had taken his leave.

"One last hand, then?" Clint asked.

"Agreed," Lanigan said.

Brennan nodded. He had the deal.

The final hand of the night went to Lanigan. No surprise. He was the winner of the day.

"A beer?" he asked them. "On me?"

"Not for me, thanks," Brennan said. "My wife's waitin'."

"You have a wife?" Clint asked.

"I never said?"

"No," Lanigan said.

"Well," he said, "I don't know how much longer I'll have her. She's about fed up." He waved. "See you gents tomorrow."

As he left, Clint and Lanigan went to the bar.

"Beer?" Jasper asked.

Lanigan nodded.

"On me," Clint said.

"No," Lanigan said, "I won, I'll pay."

"Okay."

Jasper drew the beers and set them down.

"Sorry about the three jacks," Lanigan said.

"I knew you had them," Clint said, "I just couldn't bring myself to fold three tens."

"It would have been a hell of a fold."

"Wilkins outplayed me that hand," Clint pointed out. "He folded his three of a kind."

"He didn't outplay you," Lanigan said. "He lacked the gall to play the hand."

"Still," Clint said. "He lost less money than I did."

"I can't argue that."

They clinked glasses and finished their beers.

NINE

Clint rose in the morning, kicked the fire to death, and saddled Eclipse. It was time to go and find some supplies. As he rode, he remembered that last day in El Legado . . . the one that had led him here . . .

He rose that morning, like others, rolled over to find Jenny there. She had taken to spending each night with him. He hoped she hadn't gotten too used to it. He'd be leaving town soon.

He got dressed and went down to the lobby. His intention was to have breakfast, but when he got there, he saw the sheriff coming through the front door with two young deputies.

"Sheriff," Clint said.

"Stand fast, Adams," the lawman said.

"What?"

"Don't make any quick moves," Cox said. "We'll need your gun."

"You'll need my—what?"

The two deputies' hands hovered over their weapons.

"Tell them not to skin those hoglegs, Sheriff," Clint said. "Don't give me a reason . . ."

"Take it easy, boys," Cox said, holding his hand out. "Don't touch your guns."

"What is this all about?"

"If you'll come with me to my office, I'll tell you," Cox said. "Please."

"All right," Clint said, "but I'm not giving up my gun."

"That's okay," Cox said, "for now."

They left the hotel, the deputies trailing nervously behind.

In the sheriff's office, Cox said, "Have a seat."

"I'll stand," Clint said, "and I don't want them behind me."

"Stand over here, boys," Cox said, pointing.

They stood to either side of his desk as he sat.

"Now what's this about?"

"Your friend, Lanigan," Cox said.

"What about him?"

"He's dead."

"What?" Clint asked. "When? How?"

"Last night," Cox said. "Somebody shot him."

"In the back?"

"No," Cox said, "the chest."

"Are you suggesting that I did it?"

"Well," Cox said, "he took a big hand from you last night. Everybody saw it."

"That's just poker," Clint said. "That's nothing to kill over. What about Creed?"

"Well . . . if he had been shot in the back, maybe," Sheriff Cox said.

"Have you talked to him?"

"Not yet."

"You mean, you came after me first?"

"Well," the lawman said, "your reputation . . ."

"I had no reason to kill Lanigan," Clint said.

"I'm just doing my job, Adams," Cox said. "I'll talk to Creed, and then I'll have to make up my mind."

"Were there any witnesses?"

"Not that I've found yet."

"Where did it happen?"

"In front of his rooming house."

"And nobody heard anything?"

The sheriff didn't answer.

"Wait," Clint said, "you mean you actually haven't spoken to anybody? You came after me first?"

"Like I said," Cox replied, "your reputation."

"Okay," Clint said, "I'm done here." He stood up and headed for the door.

"Do me a favor, Adams," Cox said.

"What's that?"

"Don't leave town."

"I won't," Clint said, then added, "not until I have a reason to."

Clint went outside and stopped. Everything in town looked the same, but felt different. There was a killer there, and just as Sheriff Cox had thought of him first, he was thinking of Johnny Creed first. But before he talked to the young man, he decided to go over to the rooming house.

* * *

After Clint Adams left the sheriff's office, one of the deputies said to Cox, "What do we do, Sheriff?"

"Keep an eye on him," Cox said. "Let me know if he leaves town."

Neither deputy moved.

"Which one of us?" Tom Getty asked.

"Both of you," Cox said. "Take turns."

"What if he sees us?" Jesse Watts asked nervously.

"He will," Cox said. "In fact, he'll expect to see you. Don't worry. He won't do anything."

"Are you sure?"

"Positive," Cox said. "Just don't go anywhere near your guns."

Both deputies swallowed hard.

"Go on," Cox said. "You can decide between you who should go first."

"What are you gonna do?"

"My job," Cox said. "I'm going to try to find out who shot Lanigan."

TEN

When Clint knocked on the door of Erin O'Shea's rooming house, the woman herself answered, holding a white hanky to her face.

"You!" she said. "You have a nerve, comin' here."

"Mrs. O'Shea," he said, "I just heard about Lanigan. I wanted to ask you—"

"Why would I let you in my house?" she demanded.

"Why wouldn't you?" he asked. "I only want to talk."

"But—but—but . . . you shot him!" she exclaimed.

"What?" he said. "Who told you that? Where did you hear that?"

"Everywhere!" she said. "It's all over town that the Gunsmith shot Mr. Lanigan."

"I don't know who's passing that around, ma'am," he said, "but I most certainly didn't shoot Lanigan. I don't make a habit of shooting my friends."

"Then—then why would anyone say that?"

"I can only guess," he said, "that the person who is saying I killed him is actually the killer."

She said, "Oh!"

"Do you know who it is?"

"Why, no," she said. "I just heard it from . . . some of the boarders at breakfast."

"Ma'am," he said, "would those boarders be home now?"

"Um, no," she said, "there's no one in the house right now. Mr. Lanigan was the only one who used to . . . stay around during the day."

"Well, could you give me their names?"

"You're not going to . . . hurt them, are you?"

"No, ma'am," Clint said. "I'd just like to find out who's spreading those lies about me, and I'd also like to find out who actually killed Mr. Lanigan."

"Isn't that the sheriff's job?" she asked.

"No, ma'am," Clint said. "Not when somebody is spreading the word that I did it. Then it becomes my job."

"Oh," she said, "well, come in then."

She allowed him to enter and led him to the living room once again.

"Ma'am—"

"Please," she said, "just call me Erin."

"All right," he said. "Erin, I heard that Lanigan was shot in front of the house. Did you hear anything?"

"I don't understand it," she said. "I heard nothing."

"Did anyone else hear anything?"

"I—I don't know," she said. "You would have to ask them."

"How many boarders do you have?"

"Five," she said, "six, with . . . with poor Mr. Lanigan."

"Did he get along with the others?"

Her eyes widened.

"You think perhaps one of them did it?"

"I don't know," he said, "but I'm going to have to ask."

"Oh my God," she said, "the very thought that I might have a . . . a killer staying in my house—"

"Don't jump to any conclusions, ma—Erin," Clint said. "I'm just going to ask some questions."

"I'll give you their names, if you think it will help find who killed Mr. Lanigan. He was such a nice man."

"Yes, he was," Clint said. "And thank you for believing that I didn't kill him."

"After you were here that time," she said, "he spoke very highly of you. I got the impression that you were friends."

"I'd like to think we were."

"I still can't believe it," she said, sitting on the sofa and once again lifting her hanky to her face.

"Well," he said awkwardly, "if you'll let me have those names, I'll leave you to your, uh, grief."

"Oh, yes," she said. "Of course. Shall I write them down for you?"

"Please," he said, "and if you can give me some hint about where to find them, that would be great."

"Of course," she said, standing. "I'll be right back."

He waited there while she left the room, wondering how close Lanigan had gotten with his landlady.

Clint left the house armed with the names of her boarders, and some idea of where to find them. She also told him which ones had said that it was the Gunsmith who'd killed Lanigan.

But before he went looking for them, he went to Dan Brennan's general store and was surprised to find him there.

"Gotta come into work sometime," Brennan said. "I'm tryin' to keep the wife happy—sort of."

"Did you hear about Lanigan?"

"Gettin' killed? Yeah, I heard it."

"The word's going around town that I did it."

"That's what I heard," Brennan said, "but I don't see any reason for it."

"There isn't any reason, because I didn't do it."

"I believe you."

"Do you have any idea who did?"

"Well, I don't wanna point the finger . . ." the man said.

"Go ahead," Clint said, "point it."

"Okay. If he'd been shot in the back, I'd be lookin' at Johnny Creed. But I heard he was shot in the chest."

"That's what I heard, too."

"So I guess he coulda been bushwhacked."

"Do you know where I can find Creed?"

"His family had a house outside of town," he said. "I suppose he still lives there."

"Tell me how to get there. Do I need my horse?"

"Naw, you can walk," Brennan said. "It's . . ."

ELEVEN

Clint found all of Erin O'Shea's boarders. None of them had heard anything outside the house either the night before or that morning. Pete Nixon had told her at breakfast that the Gunsmith had shot Lanigan over a poker hand.

"Who told you that?" Clint asked him. He'd found Nixon working on the printing press at the town newspaper. Apparently that was his job, traveling from town to town doing repairs.

"I don't know," the man said from under the press. "Somebody."

Clint leaned down, grabbed his legs, and pulled him out from under the thing.

"I'm talking to you," he said. "Stand up and look at me."

"What's the problem?" the man asked. He stood, towering over Clint, but almost emaciated. "Why's it so important to you who told me the Gunsmith killed the gambler?"

"Because," Clint said. "I am the Gunsmith."

The color drained from the man's face, making him look more forty than his real age of thirty.

"Oh, uh," the man said, "s-sorry. I just, uh, heard it someplace."

"Okay, I know that already," Clint said. "I want to know where you heard it. It was early this morning, before you even had breakfast. Where did you go?"

"For a walk."

"Where?'

"Into town."

"Did you stop anywhere?"

"No."

"Then how did you hear it?"

"On the street," Nixon said. "People were just talking about it."

"What people?"

"I don't know," Nixon said, "just people on the street. I don't know nobody's name."

Clint got it. The word had hit the street. But he needed to know who started it.

"Can I, uh, go back to work now?" the man asked.

"Yeah, sure," Clint said. "Go ahead."

The young man got on the floor, but before he slid under the press, he looked up at Clint and asked, "So you didn't kill the gambler?"

"No," Clint said, "I didn't."

He left the newspaper office and went back to the sheriff's office. Cox was there without his deputies, but Clint knew where one of them was—right behind him.

"Back so soon?" Cox asked.

"You find out anything yet?"

"No," Cox said, "you?"

"Just that people on the street are spreading the word that I killed Lanigan," Clint said. "I'd like to find out who started that story."

"Well," Cox said, "I'm tryin' to find out who killed the gambler. Maybe when I do that, I'll find out."

"But you still think I did it."

"I think it's possible."

"Okay," Clint said, "so I need to do this myself."

"Just don't leave town, Mr. Adams."

"I'll remember."

He left the office, walked down the street with the young deputy behind him.

He went to the undertaker's office next.

"Have you lost a loved one?" the man asked as Clint entered. He was gray-haired, in his sixties, wearing a gray suit instead of the traditional black.

"No," Clint said, "not a loved one. Just a friend. The gambler that was shot this morning."

"Ah, Mr. Lanigan, yes. Will you be paying for his burial?"

"What? Paying—yes, yes, I will. I'll pay."

"Then you've come to pick out a casket and a marker."

"Sure, I'll do that," Clint said. "But first I want to see the body."

"Of course," the man said, "one last viewing. This way."

He led Clint into a back room where Lanigan was laid out on a table.

"Give me a minute?"

"Sure."

The man left.

Clint walked to the table and stared down at Lanigan. There was a neat hole in his chest. The bullet would certainly have exploded his heart.

"Too bad you were so busy watching your back," Clint said. "I guess you didn't see it coming from the front."

Or maybe he did see it coming, and it was someone he knew, someone he didn't fear. But this wasn't his town. Who could that have been? Only somebody from the boardinghouse, or somebody from the poker game.

Clint couldn't think of anyone in the game who would want to kill Lanigan. At least, none of the local businessmen. Maybe Creed . . . or someone from the house.

But he had talked to the other boarders. They were all passing through town, had never met Lanigan before. Who would have had a motive to kill him?

Two of the boarders were men under thirty, one was in his forties, the other two were older. Maybe somebody knew that the landlady was sweet on Lanigan, and was jealous?

To find that out, he'd have to talk to the lovely landlady, Mrs. O'Shea, again.

TWELVE

He found Mrs. O'Shea with a cloth in her hand, dusting her living room.

"Oh, you're back," she said. "Did you find out anything?"

"I think Lanigan was shot by somebody he knew," Clint said.

"Somebody from the house?"

"He didn't know the people here very well, did he?" Clint asked. "They'd all just met, right?"

"That's correct."

"Let me ask you something, Erin," Clint said, "and please don't be insulted."

"All right."

"You're a lovely woman."

"Why would that make me feel insulted?" she asked.

"What about the men in this house?"

"What about them?"

"Do you think any of them . . . like you?"

"I hope that all of them like me, Mr. Adams," she said.

"No, I mean . . . really like you."

"What do you—oh? You mean . . . like that?"

"Yes," Clint said, "like that."

"I don't do that with boarders, Mr. Adams," she said.

"Well, you'll excuse me for saying so," Clint said, "but you seemed to like Mr. Lanigan."

"I did like him."

"A lot?" Clint asked. "More than the other boarders?"

"Perhaps," she said. "He was . . . a gentleman."

"So do you think any of the others were jealous?"

"Jealous? You mean . . . jealous enough to kill him?" she asked.

"That's what I mean."

"Oh, no," she said. "That couldn't be."

"Are you sure?"

She seemed to give the matter some thought, then said, "No, it's not possible. None of them have ever even suggested anything to me."

"Okay," Clint said, "okay. That just leaves the poker game."

"What?"

"Never mind," he said. "I'll leave you to your cleaning now. Thanks."

He turned and left the house.

Wilkins, the drifter, could always be found in the saloon. If he wasn't drinking, he was playing poker. At the moment he was standing at the bar, drinking.

"Adams," Wilkins said as Clint entered. "Come have a beer. We can lift one to poor Lanigan."

Clint approached the bar and nodded to Jasper, who drew him a cold one.

"When was the last time you saw Lanigan, Wilkins?" Clint asked.

"What? Last night, after the game."

"Not since?"

"No, why? Oh, wait," Wilkins said. "I heard some talk about you killing him."

"I didn't."

"I didn't think so," Wilkins said, "but do you think I did?"

"No," Clint said, "I can't see any reason why you would—unless you knew him before you both came here."

"No, never saw him before."

"Okay."

"So why do you want to know when I saw him last?"

"I thought maybe you saw him with someone," Clint said. "I'm thinking he was shot by somebody he knew."

"From the game?"

"I don't think any of us had a reason to do it."

"Then who?" Wilkins asked. "Somebody at the boardinghouse?"

"I've talked to everyone involved," Clint said. "I don't think so."

"Then who?"

"That's what I'm trying to find out," Clint said. "The only name I can come up with right now is Johnny Creed."

"The kid? You mean, because of what happened the other night?"

"Maybe."

"Then why don't you find him?" Wilkins suggested.

"It's what I'm going to do next."

"Want somebody to watch your back?"

"I thought you'd never ask."

Clint looked at Jasper.

"How much do you know about the kid?"

"Creed? He grew up here."

"Did you know his father?"

"No, and I didn't know his mother," Jasper said. "She died when he was young."

"So who brought him up?" Clint asked. "An aunt? Perhaps an uncle?"

"No," Jasper said. "There were none of those. He pretty much grew up on the street."

"I have directions to get to his house," Clint said. "That is, his family's house. Does he still live there?"

"I guess so," Jasper said. "I don't know of anyplace else he lives."

Clint looked at Wilkins.

"I guess we'll take a walk and see if he's home."

"Fine with me," Wilkins asked. "I kinda liked Lanigan. Thought I could learn a thing or two from him."

"I'm sure you could have," Clint said. "He was a very good poker player."

"You're pretty good, too," Wilkins said. "I was learning a lot from the two of you."

"Well," Clint said, "let's go and find the kid and see what he's learned."

THIRTEEN

They found the house with no trouble. It appeared from the outside to be barely livable. In fact, it looked like it only had three walls.

"Well," Clint said, "we won't have any trouble getting in, will we?"

They walked around and entered the house through the missing wall. There were empty cans strewn about, a bedroll in one corner, and on an old kitchen counter some dirty silverware and coffee mugs.

"He lives here," Wilkins said, "kinda."

Clint looked around. There was nothing there that was any help to him. Especially since he didn't know what he was looking for.

"So now what?" Wilkins asked.

"Just find him, I guess," Clint said. "He's probably somewhere around town."

"What if he's gone?"

"Why would he leave?"

"You're thinkin' he killed Lanigan, right?"

"Maybe."

"What better reason to leave town, then?" Wilkins asked. "To avoid the law."

They left the house, headed back to town.

"If he has left town," Clint said, "I'm going to have to go after him."

"I don't mind helpin' you find him here in town," Wilkins said, "but I can't—"

"No," Clint said, cutting him off, "I'm not asking you to go with me."

"Oh," Wilkins said, "okay."

They reached town and separated. If Wilkins saw the kid, Creed, he'd find Clint and tell him about it. He had no reason to brace him. That was up to Clint.

Clint was crossing the street, about to check one of the saloons for Creed, when he saw Sheriff Cox coming toward him, flanked by his two deputies.

"Now what?" Clint asked.

"I've got a witness," Cox said.

"To what?" Clint asked. "It can't be to me killing Lanigan, because I didn't do it."

"No," Cox said, "not to you killing him. But to you threatening to kill him."

"I didn't do that either."

"Our witness said you did, during an argument. A real loud argument."

"And where did this argument take place?" Clint asked. "And who is the witness?"

"I'm not going to tell you that now," Cox said. "I don't want my witnesses to . . . disappear."

"You think I'd kill him, or her?"

"I'm just saying—"

"I hope you're not planning to try taking my gun," Clint said, staring at the two deputies. They both looked away.

"I'll do that when I'm ready to arrest you," Sheriff Cox told him.

"Then I'll get on with my day," Clint replied, "if you don't mind."

"Just don't try to leave town," Cox said.

"You told me that already," Clint said. "What I'd like to know is how you plan to stop me if I was ready to leave."

Cox stared at him, then turned and walked away, trailed by his two deputies.

Clint decided to change direction. Instead of checking the saloons, he was going to check the livery stable.

As he entered the stable, the hostler came walking over to him, wiping his hands on a dirty rag.

"Come to check on your horse?"

"No," Clint said, "but I'll take a look at him while I'm here."

They both walked over to Eclipse's stall. Clint ran his hand over the horse's flanks.

"Wonderful animal," the old hostler said. "Best I've seen, and I've worked with horses for sixty years."

"What's your name, Pop?"

"It ain't Pop," the man said. "It's Pete." He cackled. "You was close."

"You been in this town that long?" Clint asked.

"No," the man said, "but I've been here for twenty years."

"Do you know Johnny Creed?"

"Sure, I know the kid."

"Did you know his old man?"

"Jimmy? Yeah, him, too."

"Have you seen Johnny lately?"

"Sure," the man said, "saw him about three hours ago."

"What was he doin'?"

"Saddlin' up," Pete said.

"He had his horse here?"

"Most folks do."

"And he left town?"

"Yessir."

"Is he comin' back?"

"I doubt it," Pete said. "I told him to say hi to his old man for me."

"He's going to look for his father?"

"That's what he said."

"Do you know where his father is?"

"No," Pete said, "but neither does he. He's . . . lookin'."

"Do you know about the man who was killed in town?"

"The gambler? Yeah, I heard."

"You think Johnny could've done it?"

"Sure, why not?"

"I thought he'd never killed anyone before."

"That boy is bound and determined to be like his daddy," Pete said. "He'll kill for that."

"You sure?"

"Dead positive," Pete said. "You gonna go after him?"

"I am."

"Want me to saddle him up?" he asked, slapping Eclipse's rump. The Darley stood still for it. The old man told the truth. He was good with horses.

"Yeah, saddle him up."

"If you're goin' now, you have to go without supplies," Pete said. "I got a canteen."

"I'll take it."

"I'll bring him out back," Pete said.

"Okay."

Clint waited out back until Pete brought Eclipse out, saddled, with the canteen on the saddle.

"I got some beef jerky, too. Put it in your saddlebag."

"Thanks."

Clint mounted up.

"The sheriff lookin' for you?"

"He will be."

"The boy put the finger on you, didn't he?"

"He did."

Pete shook his head.

"If you catch up to him, and he's with his daddy, you better watch out."

"I will," Clint said. "Tell me, how do you know so much about Johnny and his dad?"

Pete cackled and said, "Because I'm Johnny's grandpappy."

FOURTEEN

Clint saw a collection of buildings up ahead. Whether or not it was a town remained to be seen.

It had been five days since he'd left the livery, left El Legado. Pete had told Clint that he was Johnny's mother's father. He was not related to Jimmy Creed, and if and when Clint found him, Pete wanted a favor.

"Kill him for me," the old man said.

Clint didn't promise that he would. But he didn't say he wouldn't either.

He was out of water and beef jerky. Even if the buildings up ahead were not a town, it might be someplace he could get supplies. And it might be someplace that Johnny Creed had already passed through.

"Okay, big guy," he said to Eclipse, "let's go have a look."

Not a town.

A collection of ramshackle buildings, and no people in

sight. But there were fresh tracks on the street. There was some regular activity.

Examining the tracks on the ground, he could tell which building most of them led to. He rode to a one-story wooden shack, the biggest one in the place.

He dismounted, dropped Eclipse's reins to the ground. The big Darley wouldn't go anywhere, and if a reason did arise for Clint to have to move, he'd be able to.

He went to the wooden door, tried it, found it unlocked, and opened it. He found himself inside a small, makeshift saloon.

There was a man behind a bar made of wooden planks, and one man in front of the bar, drinking a beer. Three mismatched tables were all empty. The men were as mismatched. The bartender was fifty, portly, and bald. The other man was thin, with long hair and a beard, and could have been any age behind all that hair.

"Not your busy time, is it?" Clint asked.

"You kiddin'?" the bartender asked. "This is our lunch rush."

"You got food?"

The bartender brought out a bowl of hard-boiled eggs from beneath the bar.

"You got money?"

"Not much," Clint said, "but enough for a beer and a couple of hard-boiled eggs."

"Step up to the bar, then," the man said.

The bartender told Clint how much a beer and two eggs would be. It was reasonable. Clint expected to be gouged, since this was the only place in town.

Clint moved up to the bar as the man set a beer there for him, and pushed over the bowl of eggs.

"Two," the bartender said, holding up two fingers to remind Clint.

He took the money out and placed it on the bar, sipped the beer, and began to peel an egg.

"What brings you here?" the bartender asked. The other man sipped his beer and just watched and listened. He wasn't wearing a gun.

"Just passing through," Clint said. "I ran out of water and food. What is this place?"

"Just a mud hole in the road," the bartender said.

"Can I get some supplies?"

"I thought you only had enough money for a beer and two eggs," the other man asked.

Clint bit into the egg, chewed, and looked at the man.

"Why is that your business?"

The man shrugged. By examining his eyes, Clint made him out to be about forty.

"Not too many people come through here," the hairy man said. "I'm just curious."

"About my money?"

"Thought maybe you'd buy me a drink."

Clint studied the man, then looked at the bartender.

"Sure," Clint said, "give the man another beer."

"So you do have more money," the bartender said, drawing a beer for the hairy man.

"I do," Clint said, "but it wouldn't benefit anyone to try to take it from me."

"Hey," the bartender said, showing Clint his hands, "just wondering if you could pay for supplies, that's all."

"I can pay."

The man put his hands down and said, "Then what do you need?"

FIFTEEN

The bartender's name was Eddie. He took Clint across the
street to another building to pick up the supplies he needed.
Eddie used a key to unlock the door and they went inside.
There were supplies stacked everywhere, like the back
room of a general store.

"Whataya need?" Eddie asked.

"Coffee, jerky, beans, bacon—"

"No meat," Eddie said. "I can't keep it here."

"Fine. Got some canned peaches?"

"Sure."

"I'll take some of that."

"How about some flour?" Eddie said. "You could make
some biscuits on the trail."

"I'll take some."

"Good," Eddie said. "I'll put it all together. You need
a pack animal?"

"No. Put it all in a sack, a burlap sack if you have it,"

Clint said. "Two if you have to. I'll just hang them from my saddle. I've got to travel quickly, and light."

"Okay," Eddie said. "Go on over to my place and I'll bring it all over. Tell Cesar to give you a beer." "Cesar?" Clint asked. "The hairy guy?"

"Yeah, the hairy guy."

"Okay."

Clint headed for the door.

"Hey, you need cartridges?" Eddie called.

Clint waved and said, "I always have enough ammunition."

Across the street, Cesar drew Clint a beer and they stood at the bar and waited for Eddie.

"There are a lot of tracks outside," Clint said.

"There aren't too many other places around here to get beer, or supplies," Cesar said. "Eddie's kinda got the market sewed up."

"What about a young guy named Johnny Creed?" Clint asked. "Ever heard of him?"

"Johnny Creed? Naw, can't say I have. But wait . . . I heard of a Jimmy Creed."

"That's his father."

"Jimmy Creed's a backshooter."

"Yes."

"His son, too?"

"I don't know," Clint said. "I'm trailing him. He must have come through here."

"Talk to Eddie," Cesar said. "I'm not always here."

Clint nodded.

The door opened and Eddie came in, carrying two sacks. He set them on a table.

"You want to check 'em?"

"I trust you."

"Naw," Eddie said, moving around behind the bar, "you better check while I write up your bill."

"Okay."

Clint went to the table and started looking through the sacks. His hand was inside one of the sacks when the bartender came up from the bar with a shotgun.

"Just keep your hand in the bag, friend," he said.

Clint looked at Eddie and the double-barreled Greener he was holding.

"I'm not surprised," he said.

"You're not?" Eddie asked. "Good for you. Cesar, get his gun."

"Forget it, Cesar," Clint said. "It's not in my holster."

"It's not?" Eddie asked. "Where is it?"

"It's in my hand, in this bag," Clint said.

Eddie grinned.

"You're bluffing. Cesar, get his gun, and his money."

"If Cesar comes near me, I'll pull the trigger," Clint said. "If you don't put that shotgun down, I'll pull the trigger."

"Go ahead, Cesar," Eddie said. "He's bluffin'."

"You sure, Eddie?"

"I'm positive."

Cesar walked tentatively toward Clint, and when he came within view of the holster, he saw that it was empty.

"Aw, Eddie—" he said.

Clint cut him off by pulling the trigger of his concealed Colt. He had drawn it as he sat behind the sacks, and stuck his hand in one of the bags. He figured Eddie would try something while he was checking the sacks.

The bullet tore through the bottom of the bag and drilled Eddie right through the chest. Clint hit the floor and upended the table. Eddie pulled both triggers of his shotgun as he died.

The shotgun made a hellacious noise. The shot spread out and struck the table and the wall behind Clint.

Then it was quiet.

Clint raised his head. He saw the shotgun lying on the bar, but Eddie was nowhere in sight. He looked over at Cesar. He was on the floor, torn apart by buckshot. His blood was seeping into the wooden floor.

Clint got up and walked to the bar. Eddie was lying behind it, dead.

Clint ejected the spent shell from his gun, replaced it with a live load, and holstered it. He didn't know what to expect when he went out the door. Eddie could have had some more men.

He went back to the sacks and checked them. Everything he'd ordered was there. There was a hole in the bottom of one of the sacks from the bullet, but it wasn't a big hole. The sack would continue to hold.

He lifted both sacks with his left hand, went out the door with his right hand swinging free. There was nobody there. He tied the sacks to his saddle horn, mounted up, and rode out.

SIXTEEN

Clint camped later that day, before dark. He was hungry. He made some beans and jerky, also used the flour to make some trail biscuits. Eddie's idea about that had been a good one. Probably the last good idea he'd had.

Johnny Creed had either bypassed Eddie's mud hole, or he'd been and gone because he had no money for them to steal. Might have gotten lucky.

Clint had to assume that Sheriff Cox and a posse were trailing him. Cox had told him several times not to leave town. Once he did, the lawman would have no choice but to come after him.

He ate as it got dark, drank his coffee. Eclipse was finding enough on the ground to graze on. Once again he'd leave it to the horse to stand watch that night. He needed to get some sleep if he was going to stay alert. The Darley was better at it anyway. He tended to sense things well ahead of Clint—man or beast.

"Okay, big fella," he said, stroking the animal's huge

neck, "you let me know if anybody's sneaking into camp to kill me."

He went back to the fire, unfurled his bedroll next to it, and settled in, his belly full for the first time since leaving El Legado.

He fell asleep in minutes.

He woke up the next morning hungry. For breakfast he finished the beans he'd made the night before, along with the coffee. Then he cleaned up, stamped out the fire, and saddled Eclipse.

"You did a good job, boy," he said, patting the horse, "kept both of us alive."

He rode out of camp.

A couple of hours later he was still following the trail he'd picked up outside El Legado. There was a distinctive chink on one horseshoe, so unless Creed had exchanged horses with someone along the way, Clint was still on the right trail.

From the length of the horse's stride, Creed wasn't pushing his horse very hard. They traveled at a walk most of the time, cantered once in a while, but never went at a gallop. He wondered if the boy was riding aimlessly, or if he had some idea where his father was.

Clint decided he needed a town with a telegraph office. While there was a possibility his own description might have been sent on ahead, he decided to take the chance. He wanted to send a couple of telegrams, one to his friend Rick Hartman, and the other to Denver Private Detective Talbot Roper. One of them might have had some information on where Jimmy Creed had been seen lately, or someplace a backshooting might have taken place.

He bypassed a couple of small towns with no telegraph lines, finally came to one that did. According to the road sign, it was called Rio Diablo. There was no population number on the sign, but there were telegraph lines. That was all he needed.

He rode into Rio Diablo slowly. Riding Eclipse, he could not go unnoticed, but he was determined not to do anything that would draw undue attention.

As much as he wanted a cold beer, he bypassed a couple of saloons until he found the telegraph office. He dismounted and went inside.

"Help ya?" the clerk asked. He was an indistinct man of indeterminable age. Five minutes after leaving the office, no one would remember his face.

"Two telegrams," Clint said.

"Yes, sir."

The man supplied Clint with what he needed to write them out. Clint did it quickly. He mentioned Jimmy Creed, asked for a location, and signed it with a "C.A."

"Here you go," Clint said. He looked out the front door, saw a small saloon across the street. "I'll be in that saloon when the replies come in."

"Could be a while."

"If I don't get a reply within the hour, I'm riding out," Clint said.

"Yes, sir."

Clint left the office and walked across to the saloon. He left Eclipse in front of the telegraph office.

He entered the saloon, stopped just inside the batwings. It was early, and there were only a few patrons, which suited him. He approached the bar.

"What'll ya have, friend?" the bartender asked. Unlike the telegraph clerk, this man was memorable. In his forties, he had an eye patch and a scar, and you'd remember both when you left him, even after weeks and months.

"Beer."

The bartender nodded, drew it, and set it in front of him.

"Passin' through?" he asked.

"Exactly," Clint said. "I'll be gone in an hour."

"Nice town," the bartender said. "Folks like to settle here."

"I'm not looking for a place to settle."

"Lookin' for a man, then?"

"What makes you say that?"

"You've got the look," the man said with a shrug. "Bounty hunter?"

"No."

"On the run, then?"

"No," Clint said. "If I was, would I tell you?"

"You'd be surprised what men tell a bartender," the man with the eye patch said.

"Hey, Patch," somebody yelled. "Another one."

"Comin' right up!" Patch said, leaving Clint alone to drink his beer.

SEVENTEEN

Clint was finishing his beer when the telegraph clerk came in, waving his telegrams.

"Came in almost back-to-back," he said, handing them over.

"Thanks."

"Yes, sir."

Clint had already paid, so he turned back to the bar to read the telegrams.

"That what you were waitin' for?" Patch asked.

"Right now I'm waiting for another beer," Clint said.

"Right away."

Rick Hartman had nothing on Jimmy Creed—nothing current anyway. Last he heard, he was down by the Rio Grande, but that was months ago.

On the other hand, Talbot Roper said he'd heard something about Jimmy Creed doing a job in Nevada, somewhere around Mesquite.

Now Clint had a decision to make. Keep following

Johnny Creed's trail, or move ahead, go to Mesquite, find Jimmy, and wait for Johnny there?

Patch brought him his second beer. As he set it down, he looked past Clint, then froze.

"Law?" Clint asked.

Patch nodded.

"Move away," Clint said.

He started to turn, but a man's voice said, "Don't turn around, Mr. Adams."

"Sheriff?"

"That's right," the voice said. "Sheriff Dawson. We got a telegram about you."

"I was afraid of that," Clint said. "I didn't do what they say I did. I'm tracking the man who did it."

"And the sheriff of El Legado is trackin' you, I'm afraid," Sheriff Dawson said. "I'm gonna have to make you a guest in one of my cells until he gets here."

"Have you notified him yet?"

"No," Dawson said, "I wanted to make sure it was really you."

"And now you're sure?"

"Pretty sure."

"I'm going to turn around, Sheriff," Clint said. "I'm keeping my hand away from my gun."

"I'd rather you put your gun on the bar first."

The three or four patrons in the place suddenly caught on. They got out of their chairs and sought cover.

"I can't do that, Sheriff," Clint said. "I think you know why."

"I'm not gonna let anythin' happen to you, if that's what you're worried about."

"I'm always worried about that."

"Mr. Adams—"

"I'm turning, Sheriff."

"Don't!"

Clint turned, though, holding his beer in his left hand. Sheriff Dawson was a tall, rangy man in his forties, standing alone just inside the batwings. Oddly, he did not yet have his gun in his hand.

"No deputies?"

"One," Dawson said. "He's off on another matter."

"So you came to take me in alone?"

"That's my job. Now, I'll ask you again for your gun."

"No."

Dawson's hand hovered near his gun. He was hesitant to pull it. Clint could see it in his posture, and his eyes.

"What now?" Clint asked.

"I gotta take you in."

"All you've got to do is live another day, Sheriff," Clint said. "Turn and walk out the door."

"I wouldn't be very good at my job if I did that."

"But you'd be alive to do it."

"You won't kill me."

"What makes you so sure?"

Dawson licked his lips. His face was pale, but Clint didn't know if that was normal or not.

"I never heard anything about you shootin' lawmen."

"Well," Clint said, "I don't like to do it, but you might leave me no choice. See, I can't go to jail. I've got to be out and about to catch the real killer."

"And who would that be?" Dawson asked.

"A young man named Johnny Creed."

"Creed?" Dawson asked. "I know a Jimmy Creed."

"This is his son."

"And you're trackin' him?"

"I am."

"Does that mean you tracked him to here?"

"No," Clint said. "I came here to send a couple of telegrams. The clerk must have told you."

"He did."

Clint was impressed. The clerk had recognized him, and had shown no sign of nerves.

"You ought to stick a tin star on that young man's shirt," Clint said.

"Look, Adams," Dawson said, "come to my office and we'll talk about this."

"I can't," Clint said. "I'm already behind."

"Did you get some information from your telegrams?"

"I'm sure the clerk will tell you that, too." Clint sipped his beer, noticed that the sheriff watched that hand instead of his gun hand. He could have shot him then and there if he'd wanted to.

"Adams—"

"Sheriff," Clint said. "I've got to go."

"I can't let you."

"Then go for your gun."

Dawson firmed his jaw. Clint saw that he was going to draw it. He dropped his beer mug.

It shattered when it hit the floor, drawing the sheriff's attention. Clint drew and fired.

EIGHTEEN

Everybody in the placed was shocked.

One bullet, and the sheriff's gun and holster went flying off his hip. He was left with just the belt. He was even in the act of drawing, and when his hand got there, the gun was gone.

"What the—" He looked down, saw that the gun was completely gone. "Jesus!"

"I could've killed you," Clint said, "but I don't want to. I just want to walk out that door, mount up, and walk out."

Dawson looked around for his gun, saw it on the floor about ten feet behind him. It was still in the holster, which had been separated from his gun belt.

"Don't," Clint said.

Dawson looked at him.

"I'm going out," Clint said. "You wanna pick the gun up, then be my guest. Just be ready for whatever comes when you step outside." He figured that would make the man hesitate long enough.

Clint moved toward the door, keeping his gun out. Nobody else in the place moved to stop him.

As Clint Adams went out the door, the sheriff turned and reached for his gun. He picked up the holster from the floor, drew the gun from it.

"Sheriff, don't!" the bartender yelled.

Sheriff Dawson turned to look at the man.

"He'll kill you."

"He could've killed me right here," Dawson said. "I don't think he will."

"You willin' to bet your life on it?"

Dawson shrugged and said, "It's my job," and ran through the batwing doors.

When Clint went through the batwings, he remembered that he'd left Eclipse across the street.

"Damn it!" he said, and took off running. The sheriff might actually make it out of the saloon before he got away. What then? Shoot him?

He got to Eclipse and holstered his gun before mounting up. He turned the horse and started down the street at a gallop.

Sheriff Dawson came outside, saw Clint Adams riding down the street on his huge horse. He raised his gun to fire, but there were too many people on the street to risk a shot.

The Gunsmith was gone.

Dawson shook his head, turned, and headed for the telegraph office.

NINETEEN

Johnny Creed rode into the town of Manos de Piedras. He'd gotten word that his father might be there. He didn't know if anyone from El Legado was on his trail or not, but it didn't matter. Once he found his father, between the two of them they could handle anybody—even the Gunsmith.

He rode past the sheriff's office, knowing that was the one place he couldn't go to ask about his father. Saloons were likelier, as well as the livery.

He reined in his horse in front of a saloon, needing a cold beer to cut the dust from his throat. Looking up and down the street, he secured his horse's reins to the hitching post and went through the batwing doors.

It wasn't a particularly large saloon—though larger than any in El Legado. A quick look around the room told him his father wasn't there. He hadn't seen the man in over ten years, but he'd know him when he saw him.

Several of the patrons turned to look at him, found him unremarkable, and went back to their drinks.

Creed walked to the bar and signaled the bartender.

"Cold beer," he said.

"You old enough?" the man asked.

"Just gimme a beer, will ya?"

The bartender shrugged and drew him a beer.

"There ya go."

Creed put his money on the bar.

"Passin' through?"

Creed eyed the man a moment, then said, "Lookin' for a man."

"What man?"

"Jimmy Creed," Johnny said. "Seen him?"

"Heard of him," the bartender said. "But I don't know him."

"I didn't ask you if you know him," Creed said. "Have you seen him in town? Or heard that he's around?"

"Can't say I have."

"Then go away and let me drink my beer."

"You need to learn some manners, son."

"You gonna teach me, old man?"

The bartender was in his fifties, not exactly an "old man," but no match for a young buck like Johnny Creed.

He turned and walked away.

"That's what I thought," Creed said.

He turned, beer in hand, and leaned against the bar. Nobody was looking at him. There was a time he would have just yelled out, "Has anybody seen Jimmy Creed?" But he didn't think it was a good idea.

Maybe he was maturing.

* * *

Creed left the saloon. Somebody had told him the livery was right down the street, so he walked his horse there.

"Stayin' long?" the liveryman asked.

"Overnight," Creed said. "I'm looking for Jimmy Creed. You know him?"

"Know of 'im," the man said. "Ain't never seen him."

"Anyplace else folks might leave their horses when they come to town?"

"Nope, I'm it. Less'n they just wanna leave their horse in front of the hotel."

"Yeah, okay," Creed said. "Have him ready for me tomorrow mornin'. I want to leave after I have an early breakfast."

"I'll be here," the old man said. "I don't sleep so good no more, so I open real early."

Creed nodded, took his saddlebags and rifle, and left the livery.

He stopped at the first hotel he came to and got a room, also telling the clerk he'd be leaving early.

In the room he tossed his saddlebags onto a rickety chair and set the rifle down in a corner of the room. He tried the mattress, found it only slightly better than the ground he'd slept on the night before.

He walked to the window and looked down at the street. Just because his father hadn't left his horse in the livery didn't mean he hadn't been in town. He might have stopped in a saloon for a drink and then continued on. He still had to check the saloons, and probably the local cathouse.

He left his room to do just that before having something to eat.

* * *

Creed checked three other saloons without finding any sign that his father had been there. Before finding a café, he decided to check the cathouse.

A bartender in the last saloon he went to gave him directions to a two-story house that needed a paint job and a new roof.

He mounted the rickety front steps and knocked on the peeling front door. He wondered if the whores were as old and rundown as the building.

The door was opened by a cute girl with a pixie face but a woman's body. The filmy nightgown she wore let him see round, firm breasts with big pink nipples. His dick immediately got hard.

She blinked big blue eyes at him and said, "Can I help you, handsome?"

"Um, I was just, um, lookin' for—"

"Aw, are you shy, honey?" she asked, taking his hand. "You wanna come in?"

"Well—" He gulped as she placed his palm right on one of her hard nipples.

"You know," she said, "all we usually get here is fat, sweaty cowboys, but you're kinda cute. If you wanna poke me, I'll give you a discount for bein' so handsome. Whataya say?"

"Well . . . sure . . ."

"Good!" She grabbed his hand in both of hers and yanked him inside.

Her name—she said—was Angel, and he thought she looked like one.

She introduced him to a madam named Maisie. He told her he wanted a half an hour—he couldn't afford an hour—and she let him go up to the second floor with Angel. He watched her ass twitch as she walked up the stairs ahead of him.

She took him down a hallway with a worn carpet and opened the door to Room 5. The room was hot, the bed big, with messy sheets.

"Those sheets, that was just me sleepin', honey," she said. "I ain't made the bed yet."

"Okay."

"You all right?"

"It's hot."

"I'll open a window."

She walked to the window, opened it wide, and turned to face him.

"There!" she said. "Better?"

"Yes, ma'am."

"Well," she said, "have a seat on the bed and I'll wash you."

"Wash me?"

"Your tallywacker and balls, honey," she said. "I got to make sure you're clean."

"Oh."

"Take off your boots and your trousers."

He did as she asked while she poured water into a basin. When she turned, he was seated on the bed still wearing his underwear.

"Oh baby," she said, "you gotta take those off, too."

"Oh."

"Here, let me help."

He swallowed as she knelt in front of him. His dick was

so hard he was afraid he'd explode if she looked at it. She reached for his shorts and pulled. He lifted himself off the bed so she could slide them down his legs, and then he was naked, his hard shaft standing straight up.

"Wow," she said, "you really are happy to see me, ain't ya?"

"Yes, ma'am."

"Just sit back and relax."

He leaned back on his hands and tried to relax, but he couldn't. He was trembling as she took the wet cloth to his shaft and started to wash him. As soon as she touched him, he moaned and shot what seemed like gallons of semen into the air. Some landed on the floor, some on the washcloth, and some on the girl. He immediately felt ashamed.

"Aw, honey boy," she said, "that happens a lot. I ain't gonna charge you for that. Just relax and let me finished cleanin' you."

"I ain't—I don't think I can—"

"Oh yeah," she said, washing him, "you can. You're young, you'll be hard again in no—oops, look there, it's gettin' hard already."

She was right. As she washed his dick and balls, he grew hard again in her hands.

"There," she said, "all clean. Now I gotta clean me."

She washed his semen off her hands, then removed the nightie so that she was totally naked. He felt heat coming off her pale body. She stood in front him, hands on hips, sticking her tits out at him proudly.

"So whataya want, handsome?"

"Um, I don't know—"

"How about some French?"

"I don't—I never—"

"I'll show you," she said, getting on her knees in front of him. She placed her hands on his thighs, leaned forward, and took his dick into her mouth.

"Oh God!" he said.

She sucked him a bit, then released his cock, which was glistening with her saliva, and asked, "Is that okay? You want me to keep goin'?"

"Oh yeah," he said desperately, "please!"

TWENTY

Jimmy Creed was crazy.

He knew it. He had accepted that about himself a long time ago. It was why he was good at killing.

It was also, he told himself, why women liked him. They sensed that dangerous part of him, and it drew them to him.

Like the woman he was with at that moment, in the town of Reseda, New Mexico. She wasn't a whore or a saloon girl; she was a bank teller. A pretty girl buttoned up to the neck by day, but at night when the clothes came off, a tiger in bed.

Long and lean, with hair that was brown and piled on her head in the bank, but auburn and down to her back when she was with him.

They met when he went into the bank to make a deposit. He saw in her eyes that he appealed to her, and he was able to look past the teller to the woman. He waited for her outside, and they were in bed fifteen minutes later.

* * *

Jimmy was crazy enough to let a woman affect his decisions. He'd only intended to be in this town for a few days, but Theresa Masters was keeping him there longer. Her energy was pent up all day long at the bank, and it burst out of her at night in bed.

"Jesus," he said, rolling over in bed. "Honey, one of these nights you're gonna give me a heart attack."

She laughed and rolled over on top of him.

"Don't tell me my big strong man is tired?" she said, rubbing her crotch against him. Her pubic hair was dense and wiry, and scratched his skin in a most delightful way. His cock began to harden.

"I guess not," he said.

She laughed, raised her hips, reached down to hold him, and slid him inside her wet pussy. She sat up straight on him and started riding.

Jimmy took hold of her hips, tried to keep up with her tempo, but he was starting to feel his age. She was twenty years younger than he was.

"Oh yeah," she said, "you're so hard inside me, so long, mmmm, yes . . ."

His breath started coming in hard gasps. He needed a breather without telling her that, so he flipped her over onto her back. She landed with a little scream. He drew his cock out of her and dove into her pubic hair with his mouth and tongue. In moments he had her thrashing about on the bed in a frenzy, only he found himself holding his breath while doing it. Now he started to feel dizzy. Damn it, this bitch was going to kill him.

He came up for air, but continued to stroke her with his fingers while he caught his breath. When the lightheadedness passed, he mounted her, rammed his cock into her, and fucked her until she screamed and he exploded inside her.

He rolled over onto his back again, catching his breath. This time, she did the same next to him. But he knew he was going to have to leave town.

Goddamn, getting old was the worst!

Johnny Creed felt like a bull.

There was something about this girl, this angel, this whore, that brought out the animal in him. He spent half an hour with her, then paid for an hour more. During that time they did everything to each other that a man and a woman could do. She taught him things he never knew he could do—he never knew a man and a woman could do together.

It was an education.

"Wow," he said, rolling over.

"I know," she said. "You're like a stud stallion. I think you're tryin' to kill me."

"A young girl like you?" he asked.

She laughed.

"What's so funny?"

"You, honey boy," she said. "How old are you?"

"Twenty-two."

"I'm thirty-four."

"No, you ain't."

"Yeah, I am," she said.

"You look . . . sixteen."

"I know," she said. "I make a lot of money looking sixteen."

He sat up in bed and looked down at her, sprawled out

next to him. Her skin was so clear, unlined and unblem-
ished. Her face was the face of a sixteen-year-old. It was
only her eyes that gave her away, the amount of knowing
that was in her eyes. That was when he saw that she was
telling the truth.

"Sonofabitch," he said.

She reached up and stroked his face.

"So now you don't like me?"

"I think you're wonderful," he said.

"You're sweet," she said, "but you have to go now."

"But—"

"I have to work."

"More fat cowboys?" he asked.

She laughed and said, "Yeah, more fat cowboys."

He got up and dressed while she watched.

"Are you comin'?" he asked.

"No," she said, "I have to clean myself up."

He nodded, went to the door.

"Come back and see me again?" she asked.

"I can't," he said. "I'll be leavin' town tomorrow."

"Well," she said, "in case you don't, come see me again.
I'll give you another discount."

"Why?"

"I like you."

He nodded and said, "I like you, too, Angel."

He left, closing the door behind him. He was outside
before he realized he hadn't asked about his father.

TWENTY-ONE

Jimmy Creed left his hotel and headed for the livery. Before he reached it, though, two men stepped out into the street, blocking his path.

"Jimmy Creed?"

"That's right," Creed said. "What can I do for you fellas?"

"We got paper on you, Creed," one of them said.

"Yer comin' with us."

"Bounty hunters, huh?" Creed asked.

"Two of the best," one of them said. "I'm Glip Trotter and this here is my partner, Zack Doyle."

Trotter was a mess, in his thirties, with straggly hair and a shirt and jeans that looked like he'd been dragged behind a horse. Doyle was in his twenties, tall and gangly. His clothes looked like hand-me-downs from an older, smaller brother.

"Glip?" Creed asked.

"Thass right," Trotter said. "Now, jest put yer gun down and let me slap some irons on you, boy."

"What makes you think I'll just do that, Glip?"

"Well," Glip said, "'cause our backs ain't turnt, and you got a rep as a backshooter."

"That's true," Creed said, "I do . . . and funny thing, I don't know how I got that reputation."

"Probally 'cause you done shot so many jaspers in the back," Zack said.

"Well, see now," Creed said, "that's what's odd. I just ain't shot that many men in the back."

"That ain't what peoples is sayin'," Zack said.

"Well, peoples is wrong, Zack," Creed said. "If I was you boys, I'd turn right around and walk away."

"Come on, boy," Trotter said, "you ain't about to talk us outta this. And I know you ain't about to skin that hogleg with us lookn' at ya."

"You might be wrong about that . . . boy," Creed said.

"Don't push it, Creed," Trotter said. "Now we're ready to shoot ya where ya stand and take you in dead. It don't make no never mind to us."

"I gotta tell you, fellas," Jimmy Creed said, "it really don't make no never mind to me either."

"Then skin that—" Trotter started, going for his gun. His partner went right along with him.

Jimmy Creed drew and fired before either man could clear leather. They both keeled over with shocked looks on their faces.

Creed walked over to the fallen bounty hunters. Doyle was dead but there was still a glimmer of light in Glip Trotter's eyes as he looked up at Jimmy Creed.

"Boy, I don't know how that reputation got started,"

Creed said, ejecting the spent shells and replacing them. He holstered the gun. "But it just ain't so, you see? Oh, wait, you can't see, can you?"

Trotter died and Creed continued on to the livery stable.

Johnny Creed left the whorehouse and started walking toward his hotel. Before he got very far, though, a man stepped out into his path.

"Who are you?" Creed asked. "Whataya want?"

"Boy," the man said, "I heard you just spent about an hour with my girl."

"Your girl?" Creed asked.

"Angel," the man said. "I go see her every day, but today they told me she couldn't see me because she was with you. Why, you're still wet behind the ears, boy. How old are you?"

"Old enough," Creed said. "Now step aside."

"Nope," the man said, "afraid I can't do that."

"What's your name?" Johnny Creed asked.

"Billy Holloway."

"Well, Billy, you look about twenty-five to me," Johnny Creed said. "You wanna make it to twenty-six, you better stand aside."

Holloway regarded Johnny with disdain and said, "I don't know what my girl could see in a kid like you."

"Well," Johnny said, "I'm done with her so why don't you just go and ask her."

Johnny started to walk around Holloway, but the man moved to block him again. He was wearing a worn Colt on his hip, and Johnny doubted he could use it.

"You're makin' a mistake, Billy," Johnny Creed said. "Stand aside."

"I think I'm gonna pound you into the ground."

"Look, you're bigger and older than me," Johnny said. "You probably can pound me into the ground, but I ain't just gonna stand here and let you do it."

"Get ready for a whuppin'," Holloway said, advancing on Johnny.

"No," Johnny said, stepping back, "get ready to die."

Both men kept moving, Holloway forward, and Johnny Creed backward.

"Stand still and fight," Holloway said.

"Stand still and draw your gun."

They stared at each other.

"Real men fight with their fists," Holloway said.

"Not when they're outmatched," Johnny said. "I ain't lettin' you lay a hand on me. I'll kill you first."

Holloway stared at Johnny Creed for a long moment, then frowned.

"You're crazy."

"That might be right," Johnny said. "Right now I think I really want to kill you, so come on. Try to pound me into the ground. I dare you."

Holloway backed away immediately, said, "The hell with you," and walked away . . . quickly.

Johnny Creed let out a breath and continued to walk to the livery stable.

TWENTY-TWO

Sheriff Tom Cox studied the tracks on the ground, but couldn't make hide nor hair of it.

"Ballard!"

Ed Ballard came trotting over.

"Yeah, Sheriff?"

"You're my tracker," the lawman said. "What's going on here?"

They had come to a crossroads, and needed the tracks in the ground to tell them which way to go, only there were a lot of tracks—wagon and horse—to choose from.

Ballard got down on one knee.

"This ain't easy, Sheriff," he said.

"Well, do the best you can."

Cox walked back to the rest of the posse, left Ballard to do what he did best.

"What's goin' on, Sheriff?" Deputy Will Teller asked.

"We got a mess of tracks," Cox said.

"Ballard'll pick him out," Dan Davis said. "He's a helluva tracker."

Davis was a storekeeper who'd volunteered for the posse. Two other members of the ten-man posse were also storekeepers.

"What if he don't?" Deputy Hal Toarke asked. "We gonna split up?"

"No, we're not going to split up," Cox said. He didn't trust either of his deputies to lead a posse. Teller was in his twenties, too young. Toarke was in his thirties, but was too dumb.

Cox looked over at Ballard, who was walking the roads, first one, then the other.

"Sheriff!"

Cox trotted over.

"You find him?"

"This way," Ballard said, pointing.

"You sure?"

"Look at it." Ballard went down on one knee and pointed.

"I see it," Cox said. "It's a track."

"It's huge," Ballard said, standing up. "The biggest one here. That's got to be him."

"Okay, then," Cox said. "We follow this road."

"Where does it lead?" Ballard asked.

"I was hoping you'd know," Cox said. "I don't get out this far from town very often."

"Neither do I."

They walked back to the posse to ask the rest of them the same question. It was then Cox realized that none of these men had ever been this far from town.

Some posse.

"Mount up, Ballard," Cox said, "and take the lead."

"Yessir."

The tracker rode off and the others followed behind.

Clint rode into the town of Las Vegas, New Mexico. He'd been there a few times before, visited with a friend of his who had a ranch outside of town. But he wasn't there to see a friend. He didn't have time for that. Not with a posse behind him, and a probable killer in front of him. He hoped his friend John Locke would forgive him for not riding out to see him.

He'd tracked Johnny Creed through several small towns, where bartenders and hostlers recognized Clint's description of the young man. Somehow, Creed had managed to stay out of trouble in these towns, which surprised Clint, given what he knew about Creed's abrasive personality.

Maybe this town would be different . . .

Normally, riding into a town like this, Clint would stop at the sheriff's office, but he couldn't take that chance. As he had been doing in other small towns, he tried the saloons and the livery stables. In one saloon, he ran into somebody who recognized the description.

He had just finished asking the bartender in the Red Garter Saloon about Creed when a large young man at the bar said, "I think I seen him."

Clint turned to face him.

"You think?"

"Crazy kid, right?" the man said.

"What's your name?"

"Billy Holloway."

"What makes you say he was crazy?"

"All I wanted to do was fight, you know?" the man asked.

"And he didn't want to fight?"

"He wanted to kill me," the big man said.

"But he didn't."

"No," Holloway said.

"Why not?"

"I backed off," he said. "I wasn't about to die over some whore."

"This was an argument over a whore?"

"Yeah," Holloway said. "Little whore over at the cathouse name of Angel."

"Angel," Clint repeated. "So she spent some time with him?"

"Yeah," he said, "my time. I just wanted to teach the little bastard a lesson, and he threatened to gun me! I ain't no gunhand."

"Guess you're lucky to be alive," Clint said.

"Why?" the bartender asked. "Is the kid a gunhand?"

"Reputed to be," Clint said. "I've never seen his move, though."

"What about you, friend?" Holloway asked.

"What about me?"

"Are you a hand with a gun?"

"You fellas are stupid," another voice said.

They all looked over at a man seated alone at a table. He was in his fifties, sitting with his hand wrapped around a bottle.

"Watch your mouth, Hank," Holloway said.

"Don't threaten me, ya little pissant!" Hank Calhoun

said. "That fella yer talkin' to ain't just a hand with a gun. That's the Gunsmith."

"What are ya talkin' about?" Holloway said to Hank. "Yer crazy!"

"That right?" the bartender asked Clint. "You Clint Adams?"

"That's right."

"Why are you lookin' for this young fella?" the bartender asked. "You gonna try him out?"

Hank laughed at that question.

"What are you laughin' at?" Holloway asked.

"He ain't got nothin' ta prove," Hank said. "If anythin', the kid is probably gonna try him. Or his old man."

Clint took a better look at Hank. The level of the whiskey bottle was less than one finger.

"So you recognized this kid?" Clint asked.

"I may have."

"He don't know nothin'," Holloway said. "He's just a loudmouthed drunk."

Hank laughed again, a phlegm-filled sound.

"I know more than you'll ever know," he said.

Clint looked at the bartender and said, "Give me a fresh beer, and another bottle of what Hank's drinking."

"Comin' up."

"What are you gonna do?" Holloway asked.

"I'm going to have a drink with Hank," Clint said. "And you should have more respect for your elders."

TWENTY-THREE

Clint sat down opposite Hank Calhoun, pushed the bottle over to him.

"You need a glass?" he asked.

"I been drinkin' a long time, Adams," Hank said. "I know how to do it without a glass."

"I'll bet," Clint said, "but don't get too drunk to talk to me."

"I'm never too drunk to talk." He tipped the bottle and drank down several swallows. "Whataya wanna know?"

"How'd you recognize the kid I'm following?"

"I know his old man," Hank said. "Saw the kid about ten years ago. He looks about the same."

"And who are we talking about?" Clint asked.

"The Creeds," Hank said. "Jimmy and his boy, Johnny."

"How much do you know about Johnny?"

"Nothin'," Hank said. "I saw him here, recognized him. That's all."

"You didn't approach him?" Clint asked. "Talk to him?"

"Naw," Hank said, "I got nothin' to say to him."

"Okay, when was he here?"

"Couple of days ago," Hank said. "If you're trackin' him, he's two days ahead of you."

"Would you know where he's going?" Clint asked.

"Naw," Hank said.

"What about his old man?" Clint asked. "Know where he is?"

"Not a clue." Hank took a long pull off his bottle.

"Did you ride with Jimmy?" Clint asked. "Is that how you know him?"

"Years ago," Hank said. "I ain't gone down that road in a long time."

Clint sipped his beer.

"What about the whorehouse this fella was telling me about?" he asked. "The girl, Angel."

"Just a whore," Hank said. "Looks real young, so she's popular with men of all ages."

"But she's not young?"

"Younger than you and me," Hank said.

"I see. Well, thanks, Hank."

"You gonna go and see 'er?" Hank asked. "Angel, I mean?"

"I guess I'll have to."

Hank cackled and said, "You'll like her. She's real popular."

"I'll just be talking to her."

"Yeah," Hank said, "sure. Wait till you see her."

"Thanks, Hank," Clint said. He had another sip of beer, and then left the saloon.

"Where's he goin'?" Holloway asked, walking over to Hank's table. "Is he goin' to see Angel?"

Hank looked up at him, bleary-eyed.

"None of yer business."

"Hey, old man—" Holloway said, putting his hand on Hank's shoulder.

Hank shook it off.

"Get away from me, kid," he said. Suddenly, his eyes were a bit clearer.

"Old man, I oughtta—"

"You ought to what, you young punk?" Hank asked. "You let some young kid back you down. Don't try me. I seen more trouble than you can think about."

Holloway glared at the old man, then went back to the bar.

"Crazy old man," he said to the bartender. "What's he talkin' about?"

"Hank wasn't always a drunk, Holloway," the barman said. "He rode the owl hoot trail for a while."

"Him?"

"Oh yeah," the bartender said. "He rode with some hard ones in his day."

Holloway looked over at Hank, who was pulling on his bottle again.

"Must be how he knew the Gunsmith," he said.

"Yeah, must be."

Holloway looked over at Hank again. He was completely engrossed in his bottle.

TWENTY-FOUR

The madam introduced herself as Maisie. She was in her sixties, with a pushed-up, powdered cleavage, the powder making the wrinkles there very clear.

"Somebody told you about our Angel?" she asked.

"Everybody talks about Angel," Clint told her.

"Yes, I suppose they do," the woman said. "She's very special, you know."

"That's what I hear."

"Well, you're very lucky," Maisie said. "She's not busy at the moment."

"Good. Can I see her?"

"Well, of course. Wait here."

Maisie went into the parlor, came back with a blond woman who looked like a girl of twenty or so—unless you looked at her eyes. There was experience there, and lots of it.

"This is Angel," Maisie said.

"My name is Clint," he said.

"Hello, Clint," Angel said. "Do you want to come up to my room with me?"

"I'd like that very much."

Angel put her hand out and said, "Then come along."

"Enjoy yourself," Maisie called as they went up the stairs.

In her room Angel turned to him and smiled. He could see why she was so popular. She had a beautiful body, but lots of whores did. It was her face, so young looking, and those eyes.

"I'll have to wash you," she said, reaching for his pants.

"No," he said, grabbing her hands, "you won't."

"I've got to," she said. "Rules of the house."

"No," he said, "I mean I'm only here to talk."

"Talk?" she asked. She sat down on the bed, folded her hands in her lap. "I don't have too many men who want to do that. Talk about what?"

"A young man who was here a few days ago," Clint said. "His name is Johnny Creed."

"There was a Johnny," she said with a shrug. "He didn't tell me his last name."

"Did he tell you where he was going?"

"We didn't really talk much," she said. "Except for instructions."

"Instructions?"

She smiled. "He wasn't very experienced."

"I see."

"But he was young," she said. "He was very . . . he lasted a long time. So we didn't talk that much."

"I see," he said. "So he never said where he was going when he left here?"

"No."

"Never talked about his father?"

"Never talked about any family."

"Yes, all right," Clint said. He took out some money and put it on the table next to the bed.

"Are you leaving?" she asked.

"Yes."

She reached up and dropped the straps that were holding her gown. It fell to her waist, revealing her pale, beautiful breasts. The pink nipples were already hard.

"Are you sure?"

His mouth went dry, but he'd never paid a whore before—for sex anyway—and he didn't intend to start now.

"Yes, I'm sure," he said.

"Will you tell Maisie—"

"Don't worry," he said. "I'll tell her you were great. Good-bye, Angel."

She didn't bother to cover herself.

"Good-bye."

He went back downstairs, where Maisie saw him in the hall.

"Finished already?" she asked.

Clint smiled at her as he walked toward the front door.

"I guess I'm not as young as I used to be," he said.

She laughed and said, "None of us are, dearie."

TWENTY-FIVE

Clint left Las Vegas after talking with Angel. He continued to ride west, picked up what looked like Johnny Creed's trail just outside town. He rode within hailing distance of John Locke's ranch, but didn't stop.

No time.

The posse rode into Las Vegas, dismounted. Sheriff Cox went to the sheriff's office, introduced himself to Sheriff Dave Malcolm.

"What brings you to my town?" Malcolm asked. He was tall, thin, in his forties. He didn't think the portly Cox looked the type to head a posse.

"I'm trackin' a man," Cox said. "Clint Adams."

"The Gunsmith?"

"That's right."

"What'd he do?"

"There was a killing in town that I'm looking into," Cox said, "and I told him not to leave town."

"And he did."

Cox nodded.

"How many in your posse?"

"Ten."

"Well . . . he was here."

"He was? When?"

"Couple of days ago."

"Did you see him?" Cox asked. "I sent telegrams out about holding him—"

"Yeah, you did, that's right," Malcolm said, "but I didn't see him."

"Then how do you know he was here?"

"I heard it from the bartender at the Red Garter."

"Did he say where he was going when he left?"

"You'll have to ask the bartender at the Red Garter," Malcolm said.

"I'll do that," Cox said, starting for the door.

"Sheriff, I'd appreciate it if you'd keep your posse in line while you're here," Malcolm said.

"Don't worry, Sheriff Malcolm," Sheriff Cox said, "my boys will be good."

"How long you plan on being here?"

"Just long enough to get a line on where Adams was going." He grabbed the doorknob.

"By the way . . ."

"Yeah?"

"Is he runnin' from you," Malcolm asked, "or is he lookin' for somebody?"

"Why? What did you hear?"

"Not much," Malcolm said. "Talk to the bartender—"

"At the Red Garter," Cox said. "Yes, I know. Thanks." He went out.

*   *   *

Outside, Deputy Teller asked, "Any sign on him?"

"He was here a couple of days ago," Cox said.

"And where'd he go?"

"Don't know that," Cox said.

"Who does?" Deputy Toarke asked.

"Apparently, he talked to the bartender at the Red Garter," Cox said.

"Okay," one of the other men said, "let's go to the saloon."

"We're going," Cox said, "but you men are staying outside."

"Sheriff," one of them said, "we've got some dust to cut."

"Cut it with water, Ames," Cox said. "Teller, you'll come inside with me. Toarke, stay outside with the rest of the men and keep them in line."

"Yessir."

Cox mounted up and they all rode to the Red Garter.

In the Red Garter, a man was standing at the bar with the bartender, nursing a beer. It was early, and there were only a few others in the place.

Sheriff Cox and Deputy Teller walked in and looked around, then approached the bar.

"Help ya, Sheriff?" the bartender asked.

"I heard you had Clint Adams in here a while back," Cox said. "I'm looking for him."

"Matter of fact," the bartender said, "he was here a day or two ago, but he ain't here now."

"I know that," Cox said. "I want to know if he told you where he was going when he left here."

"When he left here?" the bartender asked.

"That's right."

"Well," the man said, "when he left this here saloon, he was going to the whorehouse. It's called Maisie's."

"Maisie's?"

"That's right."

"He went to a whorehouse?" Teller asked.

"Yep."

"Why?" Cox asked.

"Sheriff," the barman said, "why would anyone go to a whorehouse?"

Cox and Teller exchanged a glance, before the sheriff looked back at the bartender and asked, "Did he talk to anyone else while he was here?"

"Well, yeah," the barman said, "he talked to Billy here, and he talked to Hank over there."

"Hank?"

"Fella with his head down on the table," the bartender said.

Cox looked at Billy.

"What do you do, young fella?"

"He don't do a thing," the barman said.

"I do odd jobs," Holloway said.

"What did Clint Adams have to say to you?"

"Not much."

"He told him to shut up," the bartender said. "Fact is, Adams talked more to Hank."

"Hank."

The bartender nodded.

"That man," Cox said, pointing.

"Yep."

"Was he awake at the time?"

"Ol' Hank knows what he's talkin' about," the bartender said.

"He's a damn drunk!" Holloway said.

"And what are you doing in here this early in the day?" Sheriff Cox asked.

"Yeah," the bartender said.

"Can I wake him up?" Cox asked.

The bartender put a bottle of whiskey on the bar and said, "Try this."

The sheriff reached for it, but the barman pulled it back.

"Right," Cox said. He put some money on the bar and the bartender gave him the bottle.

"Stay here," Cox said to Teller. He took the bottle and walked over to Hank's table.

TWENTY-SIX

Jimmy Creed crossed from New Mexico into Arizona. He was looking for a place to light and set for a while. He was tired of riding from town to town, but he needed a place where nobody knew him, nobody had heard that reputation of his. Okay, so he had shot a few men in the back. He had also shot a lot of them in the chest.

In his fifties, he was hurting from the long ride—his ass was hurting from the saddle, his back was hurting from sleeping on the ground, and his stomach was hurting from trail coffee and jerky.

Maybe this next town was the one.

Johnny Creed rode into Reseda, New Mexico, having followed his father's trail there.

When he left El Legado, he didn't know if he'd be able to pick up his old man's trail. He followed rumors about where Jimmy Creed had been seen, and amazingly, he did pick up the trail. And it led him here.

Johnny wasn't on the run, so he had no problem checking in with the local sheriff to ask about his father. He reined his horse in and entered the office.

"Help you, son?" the white-haired lawman asked.

"I'm looking for Jimmy Creed, Sheriff. Did he pass through here?"

"He not only passed through," the sheriff said, "he killed two men while he was here."

"Did he shoot them in the back?"

"Hello, no," the lawman said. "Face-to-face."

"Are you after him for that?"

"Not at all," the man said. He had a big chaw of tobacco in his mouth, and he leaned over to spit a small wad of it into a spittoon. "Seems like it was a fair fight to me."

"Really?"

"Boy, you believe all them stories about Jimmy Creed shootin' men in the back?" the man asked. "I hear he shot at least as many in the front."

"I never heard that."

"What's your interest?" the sheriff asked. "You're pretty young to be a bounty hunter."

"I ain't no bounty hunter," Johnny said. "He's my pa."

"That's so?"

"Yeah. You got any idea where he went when he left here?" Johnny asked.

"I've got no idea," the sheriff said. "Seems to me, though, he went west."

"I've been trailin' him west."

"Why?"

"I tol' ya," Johnny said. "He's my pa."

"No offense," the sheriff said, "but I know a lot of sons who'd like to kill their fathers."

"I ain't seen him in years," Johnny said. "I just wanna talk to him."

"Not kill him?"

"No."

The sheriff shrugged and spat.

"Well, I can't help ya anymore, son," the lawman said. "I don't know anything else."

"Who did he kill?"

"Just a coupla local toughs who tried him out," the sheriff said. "They got what they were lookin' for."

"They got any family might be trackin' my pa?"

"Not that I know of," the sheriff said. "As far as I know, there's no paper on your dad in New Mexico. Can't say the same for Texas, though, and Colorado, I think."

"Okay, Sheriff," Johnny said, "thanks for the information."

"Good luck, son."

Johnny left the sheriff's office, crossed the street, and entered a saloon.

"Whiskey," he told the bartender.

"You old enough?" the sixtyish bartender asked.

"I'm mean enough," Johnny Creed said. "You wanna test me, friend?"

The bartender poured a shot of whiskey for Johnny and said, "You remind me of somebody."

"Jimmy Creed."

"Hey, yeah, that's it," the man said. "He was here a while back."

"Yeah, I know," Johnny said. "He killed a couple of men."

"A couple of men who had friends," the bartender said. "If I was you, I wouldn't hang around town."

"That a fact?" Johnny said. "I think I'd like to meet some friends of theirs. What was their names?"

"Zack Doyle and Glip Trotter."

"Glip?" Johnny asked. "What kind of name is that?"

The bartender shrugged. "Just a name."

Johnny tossed down the whiskey, shuddered, and said, "I'll take a beer now."

"Comin' up."

The bartender went to the end of the bar and motioned a man over to him.

"What?" Al Victor asked.

"Find Andy Dillman," the bartender said. "Tell him Jimmy Creed's son is here, drinkin'."

"Ah, Ted," Al said, "why you wanna—"

"Zack and Glip were your friends, too," Ted the bartender said. "Go and find Andy. Tell him to bring the others."

"Yeah, okay."

"Go out the back."

"Yeah, okay."

Al left and Ted drew a beer and put it down in front of Johnny Creed.

TWENTY-SEVEN

Johnny had two more beers and another shot of whiskey, unaware of what was waiting for him outside.

"Another one?" the bartender asked.

"Naw," Johnny said, "I gotta ride."

He tossed some money on the bar and went outside.

"Johnny Creed!" a man called.

Johnny looked out into the street, where three men were standing.

"I know you?" Johnny asked.

"Naw," the man said, "and we ain't got time to get acquainted. Your pa was here a few days ago, and he killed two friends of ours."

"So I heard," Johnny said. "Zack and . . . what was it? Glip? Stupid name. Whataya want with me?"

"Your daddy killed our friend," one of the other men said, "and we're gonna kill you."

Johnny's heart started beating faster. His hands started

to sweat. But the beer and the whiskey in his system did their job.

"Well," he said, "if that's what you're here for, then get to it. I got some ridin' to do."

"You ain't gonna do no ridin'—" Andy started, but Johnny didn't give him a chance to finish.

He also didn't give the three men the chance to draw first. It didn't strike him as a smart thing to do.

The three men saw him draw, and they all made panicked motions for their guns. They were two late, however. Johnny's gun spat four times, and the three men fell dead in the street.

Johnny holstered his gun and stepped into the street. He surveyed the three men, making sure they were dead.

"Like father, like son, huh?" he heard somebody say.

He turned and saw the sheriff standing there.

"You gonna try to take me in?"

"Naw," the lawman said. "I saw them brace you. You killed them fair and square. But I am gonna ask you to leave town."

"Ask?"

The sheriff shrugged and said, "Okay, tell."

"I got no problem with that," Johnny said.

The sheriff watched as Johnny Creed walked to his horse and mounted up.

"You want some advice?" he asked.

"Sure, why not?"

"Before you get too far on the trail, you better reload your gun," the sheriff said. "You never know how many friends these fellas might've had."

"I'll do that, Sheriff," Johnny said. "Thanks."

"Sure thing, kid," the lawman said. "Good luck. I hope you find your daddy."

"Yeah," Johnny said, "me, too."

He whirled his horse around and kicked him into a gallop.

"Somebody clean up this mess!" the sheriff shouted.

Clint rode into Reseda, reined in Eclipse in front of the saloon. If and when he crossed into Arizona, he'd risk talking to the local law, but while he was in New Mexico, he didn't want to take the chance.

Bartenders, though, well, that was a different matter.

He entered the first saloon he came to, figuring anyone riding into town off the trail would have done the same.

"Help ya?" the bartender asked.

"Beer," Clint said.

"Comin' up."

The barman set the cold beer in front of Clint, who picked it up and drank half down, cutting the dust.

"Musta been thirsty," the bartender said.

"I've been riding for a while."

"To get here?"

Clint shook his head.

"I'm looking for a young fella," Clint said. "His name's Johnny Creed."

"Whataya want him for?"

"That's my business," Clint said. "Why? Was he here?"

"He was here," the bartender said. "His old man was here, too."

"Were they together?"

"Naw, they came a couple of days apart."

"And how long ago was the kid here?"

"Couple of days."

"Did he say where he was going?"

"West, far as I could tell," the bartender said. "Anyway, that's the direction he rode when he left after killin' three of our citizens."

"How did that happen?"

"Out in the street," the barman said. "Guess he's just like his pappy."

"Why do you say that? He shoot them in the back?"

"Jimmy Creed gunned two men fair and square when he was here," the man said. "Then, when the kid showed up, three of their friends tried to take their revenge."

"And the kid killed them?"

The bartender nodded.

"All three," he said.

"Fair and square?"

"Fair as can be," the bartender said. "The sheriff saw the whole thing."

"So your sheriff didn't try to take either of them?" Clint asked.

"Nope," the barman said, "let them ride out just as easy as you please."

Clint finished his beer, dropped a coin on the bar.

"Thanks."

"You trackin' him?"

"I'm looking for him," Clint said.

"Chances are you might find them together," the barman said. "You ready for that?"

Clint left without answering.

TWENTY-EIGHT

Clint stopped in the general store to pick up some coffee and beef jerky and a few other necessities. As he came out with his purchases in a burlap bag, he found a man wearing a star waiting for him.

"Hello, there," the man said.

"Sheriff."

"Heard you were over to the saloon, asking some questions about the Creeds."

"Johnny Creed," Clint said. "I'm not interested in Jimmy."

"You a friend or kin to the young man?"

"Nope."

"Mean him some harm?"

"No."

"So you're just . . . lookin' for him."

"That's right."

"Why?"

"Don't see why that's any of your business."

"What's your name, fella?"

"Don't see why that's any of your business either," Clint said. "I'm just leaving town, Sheriff."

"Well," the lawman said, "this job causes a man to have a powerful curiosity when it comes to strangers."

"Uh-huh."

"You ain't interested in helping me satisfy my curiosity about you?"

"No, I'm not." Clint walked to Eclipse, tied the burlap bag so it hung from his saddle pommel.

"Nice animal," the sheriff said.

"Thanks."

"You know," the lawman said, "I heard about a man who rides a horse like this."

"Really?" Clint turned and faced the lawman. "What else have you heard about this man?"

"That he has a reputation," the sheriff said, "as a fast gun."

"That all?"

"He's kind of a legend—"

"Okay, stop there."

"So you are Clint Adams? The Gunsmith?"

"That's right, I am," Clint said. "So what?"

"Like I said," the lawman replied. "I'm just a curious guy."

"And does this satisfy your curiosity?"

"Some."

"Well," Clint said, "I'm afraid that's going to have to do."

Clint turned Eclipse so he could mount the animal without turning his back to the lawman.

"If you're trackin' Johnny Creed," the man said, "you

should know that he's lookin for his daddy. You might just find them at the same time."

"I'm aware of that," Clint said, "but thanks for your concern."

Clint rode Eclipse out of town, still keeping his eye on the lawman, but the man let him ride out.

TWENTY-NINE

Jimmy Creed stared out the window of his hotel. The main street of the town of Desperation, Arizona, was quiet. It was a small town with two hotels, three saloons, a general store, and a sheriff who had no deputies. There was no telegraph office, which suited him.

He'd been there three days when he saw the rider coming down the street. There was something familiar about him . . . and then he got it. He leaned into the glass of the window, smooth and cold against his forehead. Was it him?

He left the room and ran down to the lobby. By the time he came out the front door, the rider was gone.

Johnny Creed rode into Desperation. He and his horse were both bone weary and hungry. He found the livery, gave his horse over to the hostler to be rubbed down and fed.

"Where can I get a decent steak?" he asked.

"Café down the street," the man said.

"How many hotels?"

"Two," the man said. "One as bad as the other. But the steak at Harry's is pretty good."

"Okay, thanks."

Johnny left the livery and walked down the street until he came to Harry's. It was between lunch and supper, so he got a table with no trouble, ordered a steak. When it came, he dug in.

"I looked in the saloons first," a voice said. "Should've figured you'd eat first."

Johnny looked up at the man, his mouth full. An onion was sticking out, wrapped around his chin. He caught it with his tongue.

"Got your mother's appetite, I see," Jimmy Creed said. "Lord, she got fat."

"How would you know?" Jimmy asked. "You left?"

"I kept tabs," Johnny said. "Can I sit?"

"Why not?"

Johnny sat across from Jimmy. The waiter came over.

"I'll have the same," he said, "and bring two beers."

"I can't afford—"

"It's on me," Johnny said.

"Okay, then."

"What are you doin' here, boy?" Jimmy asked.

"Lookin' for you."

"That a fact?"

"Yep."

"Why?"

"Thought it was time, is all."

"How long?"

"Lost track. I caught up to your trail is Reseda."

"Reseda," Jimmy said. "I had a set-to in Reseda."

"I know," Johnny said. "Three of their friends came after me."

"What happened?"

"I killed them."

Jimmy smiled.

"My boy," he said.

The waiter came with his plate, set it down in front of him, then set the two beers down.

"I'll drink to that," Jimmy said, raising his glass.

Johnny nodded and drank.

"You on the run?" Jimmy asked, cutting into his steak.

"What makes you ask that?"

"Well," his pa said, "if you're enough like me, then you're probably on the run."

"I might be."

"Posse?"

"Not quite."

"Then who?"

Johnny chewed and said, "Might be Clint Adams."

Jimmy raised his eyebrows.

"The Gunsmith?" he said. "I'm impressed. What did you do to piss him off?"

"Well," Johnny said, wiping his chin with the back of his hand, "I might have killed a friend of his."

"Why?"

"They made a fool out of me in poker."

"Ah," Jimmy said. "You a good poker player?"

Johnny laughed.

"Naw," he said, "that's how come they were able to make a fool out of me."

"Yeah," Jimmy said, "we Creeds were never very good with the cards. Guns, yeah, but not cards."

"I'm kinda hungry," Johnny said.

"Yeah, me, too," Johnny said. "What's say we catch up over dessert?"

"That sounds good."

Over pie they continued to catch up.

"I made it look like Adams killed the gambler," Johnny said.

"That was clever."

"He's probably after me to prove he didn't do it."

"And there's probably a posse after him."

"I guess."

"So when he catches up, you want to try him?"

Johnny shrugged.

"You're pretty fast, huh?"

"I killed three men in Reseda."

"Were you nervous?"

Johnny laughed.

"I was scared shitless."

"First time?"

Johnny nodded.

"Like that," he said. "On the square."

"Three men, huh?"

"Well," Johnny said, "I doubt they were gunmen."

"Yeah," Jimmy said, "their friends weren't very good either."

"You think you could take the Gunsmith?"

Jimmy shrugged.

"He's probably gettin' older, but then so am I," Jimmy said. "Maybe you're the one who'll take him."

"Maybe."

They waited while the waiter poured more coffee.

"You look good, boy."

Johnny stared across the table at his father.

"You do look older," he said.

"Oh, yeah," Jimmy said. "I'm payin' for a hard life."

"Mind if I tag along for a while?" Johnny asked.

"Sure, why not?" Jimmy said. "Although I was plannin'
to light here for a while. Take it easy."

"Okay."

"The Gunsmith might catch up."

"If he does, he can't prove nothin'," Johnny said.

"Maybe he won't have to," Jimmy said.

"Yeah, he will," Johnny said. "The only way the sheriff
in El Legado will stop looking for him is if he can prove
I did it."

"And if he kills you?"

"That won't prove a thing."

Jimmy sat back and regarded Johnny critically.

"You're pretty smart, boy."

"I gotta get a hotel room."

"I've got one," Jimmy said. "Come on."

THIRTY

Clint was ten miles from Desperation, in a small town called Tyler. He had taken a hotel room for one night, so he could figure out what to do. He decided to do that when he found out that Tyler had no lawman. He figured the posse would have to stop for the night, so he could take the chance of sleeping in a bed for one night.

He left his room, went to a small café down the street for a breakfast of steak and eggs. Over the meal he wondered how long Sheriff Cox would keep looking for him. But that didn't really matter. He couldn't walk away from this, not with a murder hanging over his head. He had to prove that he was innocent of killing the gambler. He had to find Johnny Creed and prove that the boy had done it.

The pretty waitress came over and poured him some more coffee. She was blond, in her thirties, with a ready smile she gave to every customer.

"How's the breakfast?" she asked.

"Not bad," he said.

"That's a rave," she said, "compared to what most folks around here say."

"Well," Clint said, "I've been on the trail a long time. The coffee's good and strong."

"Folks around here complain about that."

"Coffee can't be too strong," he said.

"You passin' through?" she asked.

"Yes," he said. "I've got a room for the night, but I'll be checking out after this and riding out."

"Too bad," she said. She leaned over and whispered into his ear, "I haven't had sex in a long time."

She walked away. He watched her hips sway and she approached another table and poured coffee for an older couple. She glanced over at him and that was when he noticed that her smile was different for him.

He finished eating and she came back to pour him more coffee. Something occurred to him.

"Is this the only place in town to eat?"

"Pretty much."

"Have you seen a young man named Johnny Creed?"

"Johnny Creed?" she repeated. "No."

"Maybe if I described him . . ."

"I saw Jimmy Creed recently," she said. "Are they related?"

"Father and son. When did you see Jimmy Creed?"

She started to answer, then stopped. She shifted her weight to one hip and studied him.

"You really determined to leave town after breakfast?"

"Why?"

"I might be able to give you some information," she said, "but I need you to do somethin' for me."

"What?"

She smiled.

The waitress's name was Miley. She told him she was thirty-nine, and he believed her. Why would a woman admit to thirty-nine in a lie?

He went home with her and she took him right to her bedroom, where he watched her undress.

"I hope you don't mind," she said, peeling her clothes off and discarding them. "I smell like fried foods and sweat."

"And sex," he added.

When she was naked, she stood for his approval. She was full bodied, a little thick in the waist, but that was okay. She had big, pink-tipped breasts, full thighs and butt, a woman's body built for a bed.

He stepped up to her and ran his hands over her body while he kissed her neck and shoulders.

"Mmm," he said, "I love the way you smell."

He kissed her breasts, sucked on her nipples until she began to writhe in his arms, and then he pushed her down on her bed.

"I want to taste you," he said.

"Wha—" she started, but he dove into her blond pubic bush face first, sticking out his tongue. "Oh my God! Nobody around here does . . . that!"

"Well," he said, looking up at her from between her thighs, "as you know, I'm not from around here."

He pressed his face to her again, licked her until she was sopping wet and squirming, then she reached for him, pulling his shirt over his head.

"Come on, come on, damn it," she said, "get naked. I can't wait anymore."

He obliged her by standing and stripping off his boots and pants. His gun belt went on the bedpost, within easy reach, and then he got on the bed, mounted her, and drove his hard cock into her hot pussy.

"Oh, yeahhhhh," she moaned.

He began to fuck her, slowly at first, then faster and faster until her bed was jumping up and down off the floor. Luckily, she had her own house, so there was nobody around them to hear as she screamed and moaned.

And when he exploded inside her, there was no one nearby to hear him bellow like a wounded bull . . .

"Holy cow!" she said, moments later. "That was . . ." She lost her breath.

"Yeah," he said, lying next to her, trying to catch his own breath, "it was."

"For you, too?"

"Oh, yeah."

"Jesus," she said, turning to face him, pressing her breasts against him, "I needed that."

He didn't want to tell her that he needed it, too, ever since seeing the whore, Angel, drop her top and reveal her breasts to him. He hadn't had the time to do anything about it then.

"Glad to help," he said. "Now how about you keep up your end of the bargain?"

"Oh," she said, looking sheepish, "that."

"What?" he said. "Oh, hell, don't tell me, Miley . . . you lied to me?"

"Well, not exactly."

"What do you mean by 'not exactly'?"

She ran her hand down over his belly, through the sweaty pubic hair to his cock, which she took into her hand and began to stroke.

"Well, I did see Jimmy Creed, like I said."

"And?"

"I tried to get him into my bed," she said, "but I think I scared him. Or he had just had a bad experience with some girl. Anyway, he said thanks, and left."

"And went where?"

"As far as I know," she said, "he went west."

"And that's all you know?"

"I'm sorry."

She continued to manipulate his cock. Maybe she figured keeping a hold of him would keep him from being too disappointed, or leaving too soon.

"What's west of here?" he asked.

"Desperation."

"Big town?"

"Biggest around here," she said. "It's no Tombstone or Dodge City, but it's got what most people need."

"Well," he said, "I hope it's got what I need."

"I got what you need," she said as his cock grew in her hand, "and you've got what I need."

"Miley—"

"Just lie still," she said, mounting him, taking his hard cock into her pussy again, "this won't take long . . ."

Clint left Miley's house, mounted Eclipse, and headed west, toward Desperation. When he left the house, Miley was lying across the bed, trying to catch her breath again. Clint wondered how many other men besides him and Jimmy Creed she'd tried this with. Obviously, when she told him she hadn't had sex in a long time, it was a lie. She was much too skilled for that to be true. He actually didn't mind it, though. He did manage to get some information out of her.

Miley had told him she never saw young Johnny Creed. If the younger Creed had come anywhere near Tyler, he had apparently bypassed it.

He couldn't pick up the trail he had been following all along. The ground around Tyler was hard-packed, and he was not an expert tracker. So what he had to do was just continue west and hope that one Creed or the other had stopped in Desperation—or had, at least, passed through.

THIRTY-ONE

Miley had been right about Desperation. It wasn't a large town, but it was bigger than Tyler, and bigger than any of the other towns Clint had passed through recently.

And since he was now in Arizona and out of New Mexico, he decided to stop in on the sheriff of Desperation first thing.

He dismounted, left Eclipse with his reins on the ground, and entered the office.

The lawman behind the desk was a broad-shouldered, firm-jawed man in his forties. He looked up as Clint entered, sat back in his chair.

"What the hell . . ." he said.

"Sheriff, I'm—"

"I know who you are, Adams," the man said. "My name is Wade Barrett. I was a deputy in a town called Lonesome, Wyoming."

"I was in Lonesome once."

"Right," Barrett said. "That's where I saw you."

"You must have been pretty young," Clint said. "It was a while ago."

"I was," Barrett said.

"How'd you find your way here?" Clint asked.

"That's a long story," Barrett said. "Why don't you tell me what you're doing in Desperation first?"

"I'm looking for one or two men."

"One or two?"

"Well," Clint said, "if I find one, I think I'll find the other."

"How's that work?"

"Father and son."

"Names?"

"Creed," Clint said. "Jimmy and Johnny."

"Jimmy's here," Barrett said. "He has been for a while."

"Any trouble?"

"No," the man said, "and he's not wanted in Arizona."

Apparently, Clint thought, neither was he since the lawman hadn't said a word.

"No Johnny?"

"Not that I know of," Barrett said.

"Maybe he hasn't found his father yet."

Barrett shrugged, said, "So what do you figure to do?"

"Wait," Clint said.

"So you're after the boy?"

"Yes."

"Why?"

"He may have killed a friend of mine."

"May have?"

"I'll have to ask him."

"Where did this happen?"

"That really doesn't matter right now," Clint said.

"But not in Arizona?"

"No."

Barrett said, "There's some coffee on that stove. You want a mug?"

"I could use it."

"Have a seat."

Clint sat while the lawman poured two chipped white mugs full with coffee, handed Clint one, and sat down behind his desk with the other.

"You got any idea what could happen if you brace Jimmy Creed?" he asked.

"Believe me, Sheriff," Clint said, "I do."

"And the boy? Is he like his father?"

"From what I can see, and what I hear," Clint said, "I would say he is."

"Then it's my guess you won't want to have to face both of them at the same time."

"I want to talk to the boy, see if I can get him to admit he killed my friend," Clint said.

"And then what?"

"I guess I'll have to decide that when the time comes."

"You aren't wearin' tin," Barrett said.

"No," Clint said, "and I'm not hunting a bounty. This is very personal." More so than he was letting on, since he also had to prove his own innocence.

"I'm gonna have to keep an eye on this situation, Mr. Adams," Barrett said. "I can't very well give you a free hand in this."

"I get that."

"And I'd suggest you don't stay in the same hotel as Jimmy Creed," Barrett said.

"That's a good suggestion."

"And keep a low profile."

"That's my plan."

"You think you can do that?"

"I'm damn well going to try," Clint said. "It would be real helpful if nobody else in town recognized me, like you did."

"That might be the case," Barrett said. "We don't have a lot of well-traveled people in town."

"Well," Clint said, "just point me to the right hotel, and tell me where I can get a steak."

"Livery's at the end of the street," Barrett said. "Might be smart to get your horse under cover."

Clint stood up, put the still half-filled coffee mug down on the desk.

"Tell Chance, at the stable, that I sent you. He'll keep his mouth shut."

"Thanks, Sheriff."

"And maybe you'll let my wife make you a steak supper," Barrett added. "Then we can talk some more about this and about Lonesome, Wyoming."

"Sounds good."

"See to your horse, and come back here. I'll take you over to the hotel, and then to my house."

Clint nodded, shook hands with the man, and left the office.

THIRTY-TWO

Jimmy told Johnny that it would make sense for him not to leave the hotel room.

"Why?" Johnny asked.

"Just in case."

"In case of what?"

"Look, Johnny, you're a smart boy," Jimmy said. "Probably smarter than your old man. But what if Adams rides into town and just spots you on the street?"

"Then I'll face him."

"You'll face him all right," Jimmy said, "but you'll do it when the situation favors you, not him."

Reluctantly, Johnny agreed.

"What about you?"

"Adams won't recognize me on the street," Jimmy said.

"How did you know me?" Johnny asked. "You ain't seen me in years."

"Believe me," Jimmy said, "I would've known you anywhere."

"You don't think Adams will recognize you as my father?" Johnny asked.

"I don't think so," Jimmy said, "but even if he does, what's he gonna do? He's got nothin' against me, I got nothin' against him. If he rides into town, me and him will have a talk."

"What about the sheriff?" Johnny asked. "Do you know him?"

"I don't," Jimmy said, "but I know that he knows I'm in town. And I know he doesn't know you're in town. Let's keep it that way for now."

"So I gotta eat up here?" Johnny asked.

"I'll bring you some good meals, don't worry," Jimmy said. "Hell, I'll even bring you girls if you want. But if we're gonna wait here for Adams to arrive, let's make sure that when he does, we have the advantage. And we'll have that advantage if he doesn't know you're here."

"If he's been trackin' me, he'll know what my horse's tracks look like."

"I'll move your horse," Jimmy said.

"And then what do we do if Adams doesn't show up?" Johnny asked. "What if I'm wrong, and he ain't after me?"

"If what you told me is true," Jimmy said, "and what I've heard about Clint Adams is true, he's on your trail, all right. It'll probably only be a matter of days—maybe hours—before he rides in. And that's if he hasn't already arrived."

"You think he's here already?"

"I think he could be," Jimmy said. "I'm gonna go out and take a look around town. I'll let you know what I find out."

"And bring me some food," Johnny said.

"You bet," Jimmy said. "I'll be back soon."

* * *

That was that morning, before Clint arrived in town. But when Clint did ride into town, and stop in front of the sheriff's office, Jimmy Creed was across the street. He didn't know for sure if the rider was Clint Adams, but who else would ride right to the sheriff's office?

He waited for a while and eventually the man came out and rode his big horse to the livery stable. Jimmy had already removed Johnny's horse.

Jimmy stayed hidden in a doorway, watched as the man walked from the stable back to the sheriff's office. He'd heard descriptions of Clint Adams—indeed, from his own son just that morning—and felt more and more convinced that this was the Gunsmith.

When the man went back into the sheriff's office, Jimmy came out of his doorway and hurried to the hotel.

"You can see the sheriff's office from here," Jimmy told Johnny as they both went to the window. "Just watch, and let me know if the man is Clint Adams."

"I told you what he looks like," Johnny said, "and about his horse."

"Yeah, you did," Jimmy said, "but I just want you to confirm it, son. Keep an eye on that office door, and when he comes out, let me know it's him."

"Where are you gonna be?"

"Right here with you," Jimmy said, slapping the boy on the back. "If it's Adams, then we got plans to make."

"Okay, Pa," Johnny said, and he settled down to watch the sheriff's office until the door opened.

THIRTY-THREE

Clint and Sheriff Wade Barrett came out of the sheriff's office and walked a couple of blocks to the Mayberry Hotel.

"Jimmy Creed is stayin' at the other hotel, the Desperation House," Barrett said as they walked. "Fancy-soundin' name, but both hotels are the same quality—which, frankly, isn't very high."

"I just need a bed," Clint said.

"How did things go with Chance at the livery?"

"He said he'd take good care of my horse," Clint replied.

"He will," Barrett said. "Chance knows horses."

They entered the hotel and approached the front desk. A sleepy-looking man in his thirties straightened his back when he saw the sheriff.

"What can I do for ya, Sheriff?"

"This is Mr. Adams," Barrett said. "I want him to have a good room."

"Sure thing, Sheriff," the clerk said. "I can give him the best room in the house."

"I just need a regular room," Clint said, "preferably one overlooking the street."

"Yes, sir," the clerk said. "If you'll just sign the register, please?"

Clint signed in. The clerk looked at the full name, and his surprise registered on his face.

"Here's your key, sir."

Clint shifted his saddlebags on his shoulder and accepted the key.

"Thanks."

"Get yourself settled," the sheriff said. "I'll come and get you and take you to my place for a home-cooked meal."

"Sounds great."

"And then we'll talk more about the Creeds," Barrett said.

"Suits me," Clint said. "See you later."

He went up to his room as the sheriff left the hotel.

Johnny Creed turned from the window and looked at his father.

"It's him."

"You're sure?"

"That's the Gunsmith, Pa," Johnny said.

"Good," Jimmy said, "good. He's here." He took Johnny by the shoulders. "This is where you grow up, boy."

"Are we gonna ambush him?"

Jimmy looked shocked.

"Shoot a man like Clint Adams in the back?" he said. "No, sir. He deserves better than that. We're gonna shoot him fair and square, face-to-face."

"We?"

"That's right," Jimmy said. "You and me, boy. Together."

Clint walked to the window and looked out. If Jimmy Creed was in town, then this was probably where Johnny was headed. That was one way of thinking. But the other way was that Johnny was already there somewhere. Clint did not see how he could have arrived before the boy, after having been behind him all the way.

The Creeds were there.

He was sure of it.

Sheriff Wade Barrett entered his house on the edge of town. It came with the job, and he and his wife had been living there for two years.

"Why are you home so early?" his wife, Delores, asked. She was a short and stout woman who he loved with all his heart, and it helped that she was a great cook.

"We're having a guest for supper."

She stared at him. If looks could kill, he would have been dead in his tracks.

"You can't come home now and tell me that," she scolded him.

"You just said I was early."

"You're not that early."

"You've got to make a great steak supper."

"For who?"

"The Gunsmith."

She was stunned for a moment, then said, "What?"

"You heard me," Barrett said. "Clint Adams rode into town today."

"And you invited him to supper?"

"I did."

"Why?" she asked. "Why tonight? Why not tomorrow night?"

"Tomorrow night," the sheriff said, "he might be in a cell . . . or dead."

The look on her face softened, and then her hands went to her head.

"I have to fix my hair!"

Barrett entered the hotel lobby and walked to the front desk.

"Has anyone been in asking questions about Clint Adams?" he asked.

"No, sir."

"Are you tellin' me the truth, Eddie?"

"Yessir, I am."

Barrett went to the second floor and knocked on Clint's door.

Clint answered the door with his gun belt on.

"You ready for steak?" Barrett asked.

"I am," Clint said, "I hope your wife wasn't too mad at you for springing me on her."

"She was excited," Barrett said.

"I'll bet."

"Come on," Barrett said. We'll get home early enough to have a drink first."

As they left the hotel, both Johnny and Jimmy were watching from an alley across the street.

"It looks like he's got the lawman on his side," Johnny said.

"Once we kill the Gunsmith," Jimmy said, "killin' the lawman won't be a problem."

"Have you killed lawmen before, Pa?"

"When I had to," Jimmy said. He put his hand on his son's shoulder. "Don't worry. They die just like any other man."

They watched as Barrett and Clint walked down the street together.

"Thick as thieves," Jimmy said.

"We gonna follow 'em?"

"No," Jimmy said, "we're done for today. They're probably gonna have some supper. We'll let 'em." Now he slapped his son on the back. "Let's go have some supper of our own."

"In our room?" Johnny asked.

"Nope," Jimmy said. "You and me are goin' to a restaurant, and then we're goin' to the whorehouse."

"Sounds good to me, Pa," Johnny said.

They waited until the lawman and the Gunsmith were out of sight before stepping from the alley.

THIRTY-FOUR

Delores Barrett knew she wasn't a pretty woman. She also knew that her husband loved her. She did the best she could with her appearance, but her pride was in her cooking. She was determined that this would be the best steak dinner Clint Adams ever had.

As he entered the house, Clint said, "Wow, that smells good."

The house was small, and Clint figured it had probably been supplied by the town. But there was a woman's touch all over the inside, and the place was comfortable.

"Have a seat," Barrett said. "I'll tell Delores we're here, and then we can have a whiskey."

"Suits me."

The sheriff went into the kitchen. Clint heard a man and a woman's voices, and then the man returned with two glasses of whiskey.

"She'll be out in a minute."

Clint accepted the glass, looked around. He didn't see a table set up for supper.

"This house is pretty small, but it comes with the job," Barrett said, "We'll be eating at the kitchen table."

"That's fine with me," Clint said. "So how did you get here from Lonesome?"

"After you left, I stayed there for about six months, then moved on. I took a job as a deputy before I finally got my first sheriff's tin."

Barrett stopped, and looked inward.

"Didn't go as planned, huh?"

"Does it ever?" he asked. "I found I couldn't deal with the politicians in the towns I worked in. I ended up here, where they leave me alone."

"So far."

Barrett nodded.

"So far."

Delores came out of the kitchen then and Clint stood up. He made a fuss over her, found her a warm, friendly woman. She invited him into her kitchen, where the table was set.

It was the best steak dinner he'd ever had, and he told her so.

Later, they were sitting in the living room again. Delores was in the kitchen, cleaning up, while Clint and Barrett had another whiskey together.

"I'm figuring Johnny's here," Clint said.

"How do you figure?"

"Simple," Clint said. "There's no way I could have gotten here ahead of him."

"So the old man's keepin' him under cover?"

"It makes sense."

"Yeah, it does."

"And they probably know I'm here."

"So you think they'll try for you?"

"I think they'll do that rather than wait for me to make a try at them."

"Will they come at you together?"

"Father and son? Oh, yeah."

"What do you want to do?"

"If Jimmy's out in the open, I'll go and talk to him tomorrow," Clint said.

"About what?"

"I'll be feeling him out under the guise of telling him what I think his son did," Clint said.

"He won't turn him over to you."

"I know that."

"You want me to come with you?"

"No," Clint said, "I'll talk to him alone."

"Is that smart?"

"I guess we'll find out."

Barrett walked Clint back to his hotel after Clint thanked Delores for the great meal. He could see how pleased she was with his praise.

When they got to the hotel, they stopped outside and looked around.

"What is it?" Barrett asked.

"I felt like we were being watched before," Clint said.

Barrett looked around.

"Nothin' now."

"Yeah."

Barrett looked at Clint.

"Watch your back," the sheriff said. "And your windows and doors."

"Always," Clint said. "Thanks for the meal."

"See you tomorrow."

"Give me some time in the morning," Clint said. "I'll talk to you after I've seen Jimmy."

"Okay," Barrett said. "I just hope nothin' goes wrong."

Clint felt the same way.

THIRTY-FIVE

When the door of the sheriff's office opened, Barrett looked up, half expecting to see Clint. But it was too early in the morning. He wouldn't have had time to talk to Jimmy Creed yet.

He looked up, saw a man wearing a badge enter the office.

"I'm Sheriff Cox, from El Legado, New Mexico."

"What are you doin' this far out of your jurisdiction, Sheriff?" Barrett asked.

"I'm tracking a man and I think he may be here."

"Who's that?"

"Clint Adams."

"The Gunsmith."

"That's right," Cox said. "I've got a posse outside."

"What's he wanted for?"

"Possible murder."

"This have anything to do with a gambler, and Johnny Creed?" Barrett asked.

Cox frowned.

"Adams is here?" he asked. "You talked to him?"

"He had supper at my house last night with me and my wife," Sheriff Barrett said.

"Is he a friend of yours?"

"We knew each other before."

"I don't think you should get in my way on this, Sheriff," Cox said.

"Like I said before, Sheriff," Barrett replied, "you're out of your jurisdiction."

"He's wanted for murder."

"You said possible murder," Barrett said. "That means he wasn't tried and convicted. There's no paper out on him."

"What did he tell you about Johnny Creed?"

"He thinks Johnny killed the gambler," Barrett said. "He tracked him here."

"Did Adams kill him?"

"He hasn't seen the boy yet," Barrett said. "And there's somethin' else you should know."

"What's that?"

"Jimmy Creed is here."

"In jail?"

"No," Barrett said. "I've got no reason to put Jimmy Creed in jail. Or Johnny Creed. Or Clint Adams. They have business they have to finish themselves."

"If I take Adams in—"

"I can't let you do that," Barrett said.

"I'm a lawman, damn it!"

"In New Mexico maybe," Barrett said, "but not here. Look, why don't you go out and tell your men to take it easy, then come back in and have a cup of coffee. And we'll talk."

Cox rubbed his hands over his face, then said, "Yeah, okay, let's talk."

Clint heard the horses outside, walked to the window, and was not surprised to see Sheriff Cox and his posse ride down the street. If he had been a legitimately wanted man, he would have gone out the back door and run. But everything was in place now. The Creeds were in town, he was in town, the posse was in town.

Clint watched from the window as Sheriff Cox entered Barrett's office. The posse milled about outside, waiting. Finally, the New Mexican lawman—who had no jurisdiction in Arizona—came out and spoke to his men. They began to disperse as Cox went back inside.

Clint waited for the posse to go their separate ways, then left his room.

"Pa?"

"What?"

"You better come and look at this."

Jimmy walked to the window and joined his son. They looked down at the New Mexican posse riding into town.

"Who is that?" Jimmy asked.

"Sheriff Cox," Johnny said. "From New Mexico."

"He's got no power here," Jimmy pointed out. "Besides, ain't he here lookin' for the Gunsmith?"

"I hope so."

"Yeah, he is," Jimmy said. "You said you framed Adams for the killin', so they're trackin' him, not you."

"But they're gonna get in our way, Pa," Johnny said.

"Naw," Jimmy said. He patted his son on the chest. "Nobody's gonna get in our way, son. I guarantee it. Let's go get some breakfast."

Clint stepped out of his hotel, pulled a wooden chair over, and sat down. If Sheriff Cox came out and wanted to brace him, let him come. The man had no authority here.

But instead of Cox coming out, he saw Johnny Creed and an older man who resembled him come out of the other hotel. Clint watched as they turned and walked down the street, stopped in front of a café, and went inside.

Time for breakfast, he thought, standing up.

The Creeds had ordered their breakfasts and were drinking coffee when Clint Adams entered the café.

"Pa," Johnny said

"Relax, son," Jimmy said, "relax. Let me do the talkin'."

"What if he goes for his gun?"

"He won't," Jimmy said. "Not in here."

Clint Adams spotted the two men and walked over to them. The other diners in the place watched with interest.

"You fellas mind if I join you?" Clint asked.

Johnny was surprised, but Jimmy used his foot to push out a chair for Clint and said, "Be my guest."

THIRTY-SIX

Eventually, the three men had steaming plates of eggs and ham in front of them.

"You been trackin' my boy for a while," Jimmy said to Clint.

"He tell you he killed a man?" Clint asked.

"He told me the sheriff thinks you killed a man," Jimmy answered. "But let's face it, Adams. We've all killed men."

"I kill when it's necessary," Clint said. "Not because somebody beat me in a poker game."

"Well, it seems to me the posse's in town lookin' for you, not Johnny."

"The posse's got no power here, Jimmy," Clint said. "I'm here to bring Johnny back to New Mexico."

"We ain't gonna allow that, Adams," Jimmy Creed said.

"Jimmy," Clint said, "you want your son to end up with a reputation like yours?"

Jimmy Creed just smiled.

"You got quite a reputation of your own, Adams," he said. "You deserve it all?"

Clint didn't answer.

"I didn't think so," Jimmy said. "Well, neither do I. We all know how reputations go."

"Sure, we know that," Clint said, "but your boy's got a chance to go a different way."

"Not if, like you say, he killed that gambler. If that's true, then he's already taken his first step. So there's no going back, right?"

"You can look at it that way."

"I'm his father," Jimmy said. "That's the way I look at it."

Clint pushed his plate away. He really had no appetite to eat with the Creeds.

"You want to take this out into the street now, Adams?" Creed asked.

"Is that what you want, Jimmy?" Clint asked. "To see your son dead in the street?"

"What if it's you who ends up dead in the street?"

Clint stood up.

"Think it over, Jimmy," Clint said. "Or better yet, let Johnny think it over. Maybe he should make his own decision."

Johnny started to speak, but Jimmy held up his hand.

"I think we'll finish our breakfast, Adams," Jimmy said. "Why don't you sit and do the same?"

"That's okay," Clint said. "I kind of lost my appetite."

He turned and walked from the café.

"Pa—"

"Finish eatin', son," Jimmy said. "I think this is all gonna be settled sometime today."

* * *

After dismissing his posse, Cox went back into Barrett's office and sat down with a mug of coffee across from the Arizona lawman.

"Where'd your boys go?" Barrett asked.

"The livery," Cox said.

"They'll stay out of trouble, won't they?"

"They won't do anything until I tell them to."

"That's good."

"What's on your mind, Sheriff?" Cox asked. "How do we resolve this?"

"Well, it seems to me that you and me don't have to resolve this," Barrett said.

"How do you figure that?"

"Hell, the Creeds are here, Adams is here," Barrett said, "we can just let them resolve it. Tell me, do you really think Adams killed that man in your town?"

"Whether he did or not is not the point," Cox said. "I was looking into that murder, and I told Adams not to leave town. And he did."

"So that's the reason you tracked him all this way?" Barrett asked.

"I want to take him back with me, and let a judge decide if he should stand trial for murder."

"Well," Barrett said, "there's not much I can do about that. Your badge is no good here."

"Why are you doing this?"

"Because you're in my town, Cox."

Cox leaned forward, set the coffee mug down on the desk, and stood up.

"We'll see about that," he said, and left the office.

* * *

Clint saw Cox leaving the sheriff's office before he could blunder into him. He waited while the New Mexican sheriff walked away from the office before going inside.

"You saw him?" Barrett asked.

"I did," Clint said. "I'm sorry I didn't tell you."

"That's okay," Barrett said. "I had an idea."

Clint sat in the chair Cox had vacated.

"What'd you tell him?" Clint asked.

"He's got no authority here," Barrett said, "so unless I want to arrest you and turn you over to him, he and his posse can't do a damn thing."

"Why would you not do that?" Clint asked.

"I don't think you're a murderer," Barrett said. "At least, the man I knew in Lonesome wasn't."

"That was a long time ago."

Barrett shrugged.

"I don't figure you changed all that much since then," the lawman said.

"How did he take it?"

"Not well," Barrett said. "I think you better resolve your issues quick as you can."

"I'm trying," Clint said, "believe me, I'm trying."

THIRTY-SEVEN

As they finished their breakfast, Jimmy said to Johnny, "You did good, kid."

"I kept quiet."

"That's what I wanted you to do."

"So what do we do now?"

"We wait."

"For Adams to make a move?"

"For the right opportunity to come up," Jimmy said. "Don't worry. Our time will come."

"What about the posse?"

"They can't do nothin' unless they get the local sheriff to help."

"And if he does?"

"He won't," Jimmy said.

"How can you be so sure?"

Jimmy smiled at his son.

"Because Adams'll be dead before he can do a thing, boy," he answered.

*   *   *

Cox stormed out of the sheriff's office and went in search of his deputies. He found them in one of Desperation's saloons.

"Where are the boys?"

"Eatin'," Teller said.

"That's what we was gonna do after we had a drink," Deputy Toarke said.

Cox looked at the bartender and said, "Beer."

The man nodded.

"What happened with the local sheriff?" Teller asked.

"He isn't going to cooperate with us."

"Why not?" Toarke asked.

"I think he might be friends with Clint Adams."

"So what do we do?" Teller asked.

"We'll have to wait for a chance to arise," Cox said, accepting his beer from the barman. "On top of that, both Creeds are in town, Johnny and Jimmy."

"Jimmy the backshooter?" Teller said.

Cox nodded and sipped his beer.

"Wow," Toarke said. "The Gunsmith and the Creeds in town? We may not have to do nothin'."

"That's not the way the law works," Cox said. "You don't just stand around and watch while men kill each other."

"So what are we gonna do if the sheriff won't help?" Teller asked.

"I ain't decided yet," Cox said.

"Should we find the others, tell 'em not to do nothin'?" Toarke asked.

"No," Cox said.

"Why not?"

"Because they're a bunch of storekeepers," Cox said. "They're not going to do anything unless they're told. It's you boys I'm worried about."

"Us?" Teller asked.

"I don't want either of you getting brave, you hear?" Cox told them.

"Don't worry about me," Toarke said. "I ain't gonna get brave. Not when we're dealin' with the Gunsmith."

"And Jimmy the backshooter," Teller added.

"Okay, good," Cox said. "You boys just watch me and wait for my play."

They both nodded, and the three lawmen hunched over their mugs of beer.

Jimmy told Johnny to go back to the room . . .

"What if you run into Adams?" Johnny asked.

"Adams wants you, boy," Jimmy said. "I don't think he's gonna come after me."

"And you won't go after him without me, will ya, Pa?" Johnny asked.

"No, kid," Jimmy said, "I won't do that. I tol' you, we're gonna take him together. Just go back to the room and wait for me."

"Yessir."

Back in the room, Johnny stood by the window and watched the street. He didn't see any sign of Clint Adams, either sheriff, or any of the posse. There were people on the street, riders and wagons, and everything seemed calm. He didn't see how that could last, however.

He had given all the decision-making power over to his father, and now he wasn't sure he had done the right thing.

After all, he hadn't seen Jimmy Creed in years. Why had he just given up being his own man?

Hiding in his room, that wasn't him. And after killing those three men who had come after him, his confidence with his gun was sky high.

This wasn't right, he thought. Johnny Creed didn't hide in his room, no matter what anybody said.

He turned, grabbed his hat, and stormed out the door.

Jimmy Creed also noticed that there were no members of the posse on the street. That suited him. He ambled along the street, stopped to take a look inside the saloons. In one he saw the out-of-town sheriff and his deputies at the bar. Didn't see any of the other posse members. Experience told him that they would probably be a bunch of storekeepers.

He moved away from the saloon, since he didn't want anything to do with this sheriff and his deputies. He was more concerned with the local lawman.

He positioned himself across from the sheriff's office, settled in to see what the activity there was like.

THIRTY-EIGHT

"I think I need to get the boy away from his father," Clint said. "He was pretty arrogant in El Legado, but now he seemed willing to let his old man do the talking."

"How will you get them away from each other?" Barrett asked.

"They were having breakfast together, but that doesn't mean they're together all the time." He stood up. "I'll just go out and see what I can see."

"You think Jimmy will come after you?"

"He might."

"Well," Barrett said, "if he kills you, I'll throw his ass in jail. How's that?"

"A big help," Clint said. "See you later."

He left the office, looked up and down the street in front. Across the way he could see Jimmy Creed, watching him. Alone. Already the two Creeds had split up. All he had to do now was find Johnny alone.

He pretended not to see Jimmy Creed, turned, and walked the other way.

Jimmy Creed knew Clint Adams had seen him. Who did the Gunsmith think he was fooling? A man like him saw everything around him.

As the Gunsmith turned and walked in the other direction, Jimmy figured he'd be looking for Johnny. He smiled, thinking of his son sitting in their hotel room, safe and sound.

He decided not to follow Adams. Instead, he crossed the street and headed for the saloon.

As Jimmy Creed went into the saloon, Johnny Creed came out of the hotel. In front of the hotel he stopped to have a look around, didn't see his dad or the posse members.

He did, however, see the Gunsmith. In fact, they almost walked into each other.

"Just the man I was looking for," Clint said.

"You wanna step out into the street right now?" Johnny Creed demanded.

"There's that arrogance I saw in El Legado," Clint said. "You mean you'd step into the street without your daddy? Or is he somewhere around here, waiting to shoot me in the back?"

"I don't need my father to take care of you, Adams," Johnny replied.

"Now, now," Clint said, "if you kill me without him, he's going to be real mad. And if you get killed without him, well . . . I guess he'll be disappointed." Clint made *tsk, tsk* sounds with his mouth. "That wouldn't do."

"Whatayou want?"

"I want you to come back to El Legado with me," Clint said. "You killed Lanigan, not me."

"Prove it!"

"That's what I intend to do," Clint said, "back in New Mexico."

Johnny's hand hovered just above his gun.

"Hold it!"

They both heard the voice. Looked into the street to see who it was.

Jimmy Creed mounted the boardwalk and got between Clint and his son.

"Boy, I tol' you to stay in the room!"

"I don't need ta hide from him, Pa," Johnny complained. "Let me take 'im now."

"You ain't ready to take him, Johnny," Jimmy said.

"Okay, not by myself," Johnny said. "Let's you and me do it right now, kill the Gunsmith."

"We ain't killin' anybody unless I say so," Jimmy said. He looked at Clint. "Step back, Adams. This ain't your moment to die."

"I think you just saved your boy's life, Jimmy," Clint said.

"I saved somebody's life," Jimmy said, "but the day ain't over yet."

Jimmy grabbed his son by the shirt and pulled him away from Clint Adams.

Across the street, three members of the posse came walking along when one of them spotted Clint Adams.

"There he is," he said. "That's Adams!"

"Where's the sheriff?" one of the others said, looking around.

"Never mind the sheriff," the first man said. "Let's take him now."

"Just the three of us?" the third man asked doubtfully.

"Three against one," the first man, Webb Colton, said. He was one of the few members of the posse who was not a storekeeper. He worked at the Bar S Ranch, and was in town when the posse was formed. He volunteered to get away from ranch work for a while. "That's odds we can work with."

Denny Williams was not a store owner, but he was a store clerk, working in the general store. At twenty he was tired of being a clerk, and thought riding with the posse would give him some experience at something else. Maybe, he'd thought, he could be considered for the deputy job the next time there was an opening. Now, maybe taking the Gunsmith in with Webb and the other man—Chris Curry, who owned the town's hardware store—would get him that job.

"Let's do it," Denny said.

"Curry?" Webb asked.

Curry was thirty-five, unmarried, and his store was hanging on by a thread.

"Why not?"

He asked.

The three men stepped into the street and started across.

THIRTY-NINE

As the Creeds walked away, Clint noticed the three men crossing the street toward him. They didn't wear any badges, but he felt sure these were three members of Cox's posse.

He turned to face them.

"I'll do the talkin'," Webb said as they walked.

"Be my guest," Denny Williams said.

"This is your idea," Chris Curry said. "You take the lead."

Webb was feeling very confident—perhaps overly so.

As they reached Clint Adams, he turned to face them. Suddenly, Webb wasn't so confident, but he soldiered on.

"Clint Adams!" he said. "You're under arrest!"

As the words came out of the man's mouth, Clint noticed how nervous all three men were.

"I don't see any badges, gents."

"We don't need no badges," Webb said. "We're part of the El Legado posse."

"You still need the badge part of the posse."

"Don't worry," Webb said, "we'll take you to the sheriff. Just give up your gun."

"I don't think so."

Webb seemed confused. The other men began to fidget.

"We outnumber you three to one, Adams."

"That may be," Clint said, "but none of you know how to handle that gun you're wearing. You're all way out of your element here. And you're volunteers. There's nothing here worth dying for."

"You wouldn't," Webb said.

"You're tracking me because you think I killed somebody," Clint said. "Why wouldn't I kill you?"

One of the other men took a step back, just managed to stop himself from running. Clint had no desire to draw down on any of these men.

"I'll tell you what," Clint asked. "Just turn around, walk away, find the sheriff, and tell him you saw me. He'll take it from there."

Webb licked his lips.

"It's the best choice," Clint told Webb, knowing that he was the leader of these three.

"Webb," one of the other men—Curry—said.

"Yeah, yeah," Webb said, "okay, okay. We'll do that."

"Smart man."

But Webb was feeling anything but smart as he and the other two posse members slunk away.

Webb, Curry, and Denny Williams found Cox and the two deputies in a saloon.

"Sheriff," Webb said breathlessly, "we found Adams."

Cox turned to face the three men, who were all pale and breathless.

"You braced him?"

"Well—" Webb said.

"It was Webb's idea," Curry said.

"And you're not dead?"

"He let us go," Williams said. "Told us to find you, and you'd decide what to do."

"He's smart," Cox said, "which I can't say for you three morons. You're lucky to be alive." He turned to the bartender. "Give these three each a shot of whiskey."

The three men accepted their drinks and tossed them down. They all seemed relieved.

"I thought I could count on you men—and the others—not to do anything stupid," Cox said, "but obviously I was wrong. So now I want you three to go out and find the others, and warn them not to do a thing if they see Adams. Got it?"

"We got it, Sheriff," Williams said.

"And don't anybody get brave!"

"Don't worry," Curry said. "We ain't gettin' brave again."

"Then get out of here!"

The three men headed for the door.

"Wait!"

They all stopped.

"Before you leave, tell me where you saw Adams . . ."

FORTY

Clint decided not to wait for Cox to show up.

As the three posse members walked off, he turned and went in the other direction. The way things stood, the town was a powder keg. He had to decide what he was going to do, and do it today.

He wanted to consider it over coffee.

"What do we do, Sheriff?" Deputy Teller asked.

Cox rubbed his hand over his face, then looked at the two deputies.

"We're going to take Adams in."

"What about the local sheriff?" Toarke asked.

"Once we have Adams in custody, he'll fall into line," Cox predicted.

"You sure?" Teller asked.

"No," Cox said, "but we've got to do this before somebody gets killed."

"You think somebody else in the posse's gonna get brave?" Teller asked.

"I didn't think so," Cox said, "but those three proved me wrong."

"So how do we go about this?" Toarke asked.

"We're going to walk right up to him and take him."

"And he'll let us?"

"He won't kill one of us."

"What makes you say that?" Teller asked.

"Because we're lawmen."

"He's got a reputation," Teller said. "He kills men."

"He killed that gambler," Toarke said. "What makes you think he won't kill us?"

Cox regarded the two men, then said, "Grab your beers and let's sit down."

The three of them carried their drinks to a table.

Clint went into a café and ordered a pot of coffee.

"A whole pot?" the waiter asked.

"A whole pot," Clint said, "and strong."

"Okay."

Over the coffee he tried to work out a plan. He had to try to get through this without killing anyone—especially not a lawman. But he doubted that the Creeds—either one of them—would allow him to get his way without using his gun.

"Hey," he said to the waiter.

"Yeah?"

"Another pot?"

"You like coffee that much?"

"I need it to think."

"Most men need whiskey to think."

"Most men need whiskey not to think," Clint said. "I'll take coffee."

"Okay," the waiter said, "comin' up."

"I don't necessarily think Adams killed Lanigan."

"Then why did we ride all this way?" Teller asked.

"I told him not to leave town," Cox said. "I was still investigating the murder, and I needed him to stay in town. He didn't."

"Wouldn't it make more sense to stay in town and solve the murder?" Toarke asked.

"Look," Cox said, "it was either Adams or Johnny Creed."

"Creed?" Teller asked.

"Yes."

"Johnny Creed left town," Toarke said. "We know that."

"Well, they're here," Cox said.

"Who's here?" Teller asked

"The Creeds."

"Both of them?" Toarke asked.

"Yes."

"How'd that happen?" Teller asked.

"Adams tracked Creed, and Johnny Creed found his father, Jimmy," Cox said. "And we tracked Adams."

"So?" Teller asked.

"We all ended up here."

Toarke frowned.

"Sheriff," he said, "are we here for Adams, or Johnny Creed?"

Cox looked at Toarke.

"You know, Hal," Sheriff Cox said, "there may be some hope for you yet."

"Wait a minute," Deputy Teller said, just a step behind the younger deputy. "We tracked Clint Adams because he was tracking Johnny Creed?"

"You, too?" Cox said. "You're both smarter than I thought you were."

"Come on, Sheriff," Toarke said. "What's goin' on?"

"It's true I want Adams for leaving town," Cox said, "But I want Johnny for killing Lanigan."

"But . . . can you prove he did it?" Teller asked.

"Probably not," Cox said, "but maybe Clint Adams can."

"How do we find out?" Teller asked.

"We ask him."

Clint finished his second pot of coffee, but not before ordering a piece of pie. They didn't have peach, so he took apple.

By the time he finished, he had an idea that he hoped would work. He paid his check, and left the café.

"Adams!"

He turned, saw Sheriff Cox coming toward him, with his deputies.

"Cox—"

"Why don't we go back inside and have some coffee."

"I just had two pots."

"Then another cup won't kill you," Cox said. "I've got a proposition for you."

FORTY-ONE

Inside the café, the waiter asked, "More coffee?"

"My friends have decided to join me," Clint said. "Bring four cups."

"Sure."

Clint looked across the table at Cox.

"What's on your mind, Sheriff? I hope you're not going to try to take me in. I didn't kill Lanigan."

"I figured that."

"You fig—what?"

"I said I figured Johnny killed him, but I couldn't prove it," Cox said. "Why do you think I asked you not to leave town?"

"You asked—you told me not to leave town."

"So naturally, that meant you just had to leave town."

"I thought you were going to try to pin the murder on me."

"I'm an honest lawman, Adams," Cox said.

"I know that," Clint said. "I didn't mean—I meant I thought you thought I killed him."

"I knew it was possible," Cox said, "but more likely that Johnny Creed did it. But I needed you to stay in town so I could prove it."

"Johnny left town," Clint said, "so I had to go after him."

"When I realized that, I figured if we tracked you, we'd find Johnny."

"And Jimmy," Clint said.

"Right," Cox said, "they're both here, but we only want Johnny."

"Jimmy's not going to let him go," Clint said.

"That's where you come in," Cox said.

"You've got a whole posse behind you."

"You met three members of my posse," Cox said. "Yeah, I thought I'd need to show some numbers to young Johnny to get him to come back, but I still need to prove he did the killing."

"So prove it."

"I need you for that," Cox said.

"Did you tell any of this to Sheriff Barrett?"

"No," Cox said, "I didn't know if I could trust him. Is he a friend of yours?"

"We knew each other a while back—I wouldn't call us friends. But I think we can trust him. Why don't we go and talk to him?"

"Well, okay," Cox said.

"Hey," Teller said, "I thought we were gonna have some pie."

Cox looked at his two deputies.

"You boys stay here and have your pie," he said. "We'll go and talk to the sheriff." He and Clint stood up. "Don't leave here 'til I get back."

"Sure, Sheriff," Teller said.

As Clint and Cox entered the sheriff's office, Barrett looked up at them in surprise.

"I didn't expect to see the two of you together," he said.

"We came to an understanding," Cox said.

"That's so?" Barrett asked.

"Apparently," Clint said, "Sheriff Cox figured Johnny Creed for the killing all along."

"Then why was he tracking you from New Mexico to here?" Barrett asked.

"Because I was tracking Johnny."

Barrett frowned and said, "That makes sense . . . I guess." He sat back in his chair. "So you brought your little circus to my town. How do you expect to bring this show to an end?"

"By proving Johnny did the killing," Cox said.

"How do you figure to do that?"

"He expects me to do it," Clint said.

"With or without gunplay?" Barrett asked.

"That's up to Jimmy and Johnny, I guess," Clint said.

"You think you can back Johnny down if you face him alone?" Barrett asked.

"Maybe," Clint said. "The kid's pretty full of himself. But I'd have to get him away from his daddy to try."

Barrett looked at Cox and said, "Maybe the sheriff and I can help in that department."

"How?"

"Sheriff Barrett and I can figure that out," Cox said.

"Okay," Clint said, "get Jimmy out of the way, and I'll brace Johnny. But if he draws on me—"

"We know," Barrett said, "but that's going to be up to him, isn't it?"

"I guess so."

"Go to your hotel and wait," Barrett suggested. "Stay off the street so you and Jimmy don't run into each other. We'll send word when we've got him."

"You going to put him in a cell?" Clint asked.

"Maybe," Barrett said, "maybe we won't have to. But we'll get him out of the way."

"Okay," Clint said, "but make it today, huh?"

"Quick as we can," Barrett said. "Sheriff Cox and I will figure out a way."

"What about your deputies, and the posse?" Clint asked.

"They'll stay out of the way," Cox said. "I might bring my tracker, Ed Ballard, in on it, but the rest of them will be out of it."

"Good," Clint said. "We don't want anybody getting killed who doesn't have to."

"Agreed," Barrett said.

Clint walked to the door, put his hand on the knob, then looked at the two lawmen.

"Make it quick, huh?" he said. "This town is starting to feel like a powder keg to me."

FORTY-TWO

Clint went to his hotel, didn't run into anyone along the way, luckily. The plan sounded good to him. Let the two lawmen deal with Jimmy Creed, and then he could take care of Johnny.

He looked out his window, saw Jimmy Creed across the street, watching his hotel. Johnny wasn't with him. That was good.

He sat in the bed, took from his saddlebags the Dickens he was working his way through, and opened it.

The two lawmen decided the direct approach was the best. They left the office and walked until they spotted Jimmy Creed across the street from Clint's hotel.

"He's making it easy," Cox said.

"Let's see how easy," Barrett said.

Jimmy was lounging against a pole. As the two lawmen approached, he straightened up and smiled crookedly.

"Gents."

"Jimmy," Barrett said, "wonder if you'd mind coming with us. We'd like to talk to you."

"I ain't wanted in Arizona, that I know."

"That's true," Barrett said. "But we just want to talk."

Jimmy looked from lawman to lawman.

"Him, too?"

Cox smiled.

"I'm just along for the ride."

Jimmy looked at the older lawman from New Mexico, as if measuring him, then looked back at Barrett. Both sheriffs could see his mind working. Was it worth resisting?

"Whataya say, Jimmy?" Barrett asked. "Just a talk."

"Sure," Jimmy said. "why not?" He did the back-and-forth look again. "Which one of you tin men is gonna try to take my gun?"

"Neither one," Barrett said. "Like we said, we only wanna have a talk."

"Okay," Jimmy said. "Let's go."

As they started to walk, Barrett took the lead, Cox dropped in behind Jimmy. Creed stopped.

"You mind walkin' ahead of me?" he asked. "I don't like havin' anybody behind me."

"Sure, Jimmy," Cox said. "I don't mind."

"Thanks."

The two lawmen led the way to the sheriff's office.

Barrett had instructed a man named Owens to watch the office. When they walked in with Jimmy Creed, he was supposed to go across to the hotel and let Clint Adams know.

Owens ran across and knocked on Clint's door. When

Clint opened it, Owens said. "Sheriff sent me, said you was in the clear."

"Okay, thanks."

"You know what that means?" Owens asked.

"Yeah, I know."

Owens shrugged and ran back down the hall.

Clint put his book back in his saddlebags and left the room.

He crossed the street and entered the other hotel. The clerk looked up at him.

"Help ya?"

"Yes," Clint said, "what number is Jimmy Creed in?"

"Oh," the man said, "um . . ."

"I know," Clint said, "he told you not to tell anyone. Well, I'm telling you it's okay. What room?"

"H-He's gonna be mad," the clerk said. "He'll ask me who I told."

"You tell him Clint Adams."

"The Gunsmith?"

"That's right."

"Yes, sir," the clerk said, straightening his back. "He's in Room 7."

"Johnny Creed in there now?"

"Yessir."

"Thanks."

Clint went up to the second floor, knocked on the door of Room 7.

"Who is it?" Johnny called.

"Desk clerk."

When Johnny opened the door, Clint put his hand against the young man's chest and shoved him back. Johnny staggered backward, hit the bed, and fell over it.

Clint entered the room and slammed the door. He reached Johnny as he was getting to his feet. The boy was wearing his gun, but before he could go for it, Clint plucked it from his holster, shoved him again. This time he landed on the bed, bouncing.

"What the hell—" Johnny shouted. "You can't do this."

"Why not?" Clint asked. He tucked Johnny's gun into his belt.

"You ain't got a badge."

"I don't need one. I'm not arresting you."

Johnny stared up at him from the bed.

"You gonna kill me?"

"Not right now."

"Can I get up?"

"Why not?"

Johnny got to his feet.

"My pa ain't gonna like this."

"You and your pa close, Johnny?" Clint asked. "The way I heard it, you hadn't seen him in years until lately."

"So?"

"So why are you letting him make your decisions for you?"

"I ain't."

"Yeah, you are," Clint said. "Otherwise, why are you hiding in this room?"

"I ain't hidin'!"

"Yeah, you are," Clint said. "You're hiding here because he told you to."

"That's a lie!"

"Well, never mind that," Clint said. "I want to ask you something else."

"What?"

"Why'd you kill Lanigan?"

Johnny didn't answer. His eyes darted around the room.

"Come on, Johnny," Clint said. "It's like you just said, I'm not a lawman. It's just you and me here. You kill him because you lost at poker?"

Johnny didn't answer.

"If that was the reason, why didn't you try to kill me?" Clint asked. "After all, I beat you at poker, too."

Johnny wiped his hand with his mouth.

"Of course, a lot of men have beat you at poker," Clint said. "You're easy to beat. You're a bad, bad poker player."

"I ain't."

"Yeah, you are," Clint said. "So I figure the reason you didn't kill me is because you wanted me to take the blame for killing Lanigan. Only that isn't going to happen."

"It ain't?"

"No," Clint said, "the sheriff knows I didn't do it."

"Oh yeah? Then how come him and his posse is here lookin' for you?"

"They're not," Clint said. "They're looking for you."

"What?"

"That's right."

"Yer lyin'."

"No, I'm not."

"They can't take me."

"Why not?"

"They—they can't prove I did it."

"Maybe they can," Clint said. "Maybe there was a witness."

"There can't be."

"Why not?"

"Because I made sure there was—"

Johnny stopped short.

"You made sure there wasn't any when you killed him," Clint finished.

"I didn't say that."

"Yeah," Clint said, "you almost did."

"Get outta my room! And gimme back my gun!"

"What will you do with it if I give it back, Johnny?" Clint asked.

"I'll kill you with it, that's what I'll do!"

"Johnny," Clint said. "the posse's taking you back to El Legado."

"My pa won't let 'em."

"Your pa can't stop them."

"Then I'll kill you first, before they take me!"

"You want to kill me?" Clint took the gun from his belt and tossed it to the boy. "Be my guest, I'll be outside on the street."

Johnny fumbled for the gun, dropped it on the floor.

"Don't pick it up until I leave," Clint told him. "Then come outside. Let's get this thing over with. I've got a life to live and I've wasted enough time on you."

As Clint left, Johnny yelled, "You ain't got a life to live, Adams, because I'm gonna kill you. You hear me? I'm gonna kill you!"

"You'll have your chance," Clint called back.

FORTY-THREE

"What's this about?" Jimmy asked. He was sitting in front of Barrett's desk, Cox standing off to one side.

"We were just wondering how long you and your boy were plannin' on stayin' in town, Jimmy," Barrett said.

"I dunno," Jimmy said. "Maybe a day or two more."

"Well, the sheriff here wants to take Johnny back to El Legado," Barrett said.

"What for?"

"To face charges."

Jimmy looked at Cox, then at Barrett.

"He ain't got no whatayacallit, jurisdiction."

"That's okay," Barrett said, "I'm gonna let him do it."

"Why?"

"He's got a murder to solve."

"I thought the Gunsmith did that."

"No," Cox said, "he didn't. Your boy did."

"You can't prove that."

"Maybe," Cox said, "maybe not."

Jimmy sat quiet for a minute, then said, "What's this about? Why are you—" Suddenly Jimmy seemed to get it. He turned his head and looked at the window. "What's goin' on?"

Clint stood outside the hotel, in the street, waiting for Johnny to come out—if he came out. There was always the chance he'd go out the back door.

Traffic got thin on the street. It was clear what was going to happen, and people were getting out of the way. Clint looked over at the sheriff's office, half expecting to see Jimmy Creed come running out.

Clint hoped the boy would come out ready to go back to New Mexico. He didn't want to have to kill him.

After Clint Adams left his room, Johnny Creed picked up his gun and jammed it into his holster. This was his chance, then. His chance to show his pa he was his own man, his chance to take care of the Gunsmith, his chance to make his own reputation.

So why was he so scared?

"Sit own, Jimmy," Barrett said as Jimmy started to get up.

"What's goin' on?" Jimmy asked again, sitting back down. "Why are you tryin' to keep me here?" He looked at Cox. "Your posse—nah, your posse wouldn't try it. It's Adams, ain't it? He's goin' for my boy."

Jimmy started to get up again.

"Sit down!" Barrett said.

Jimmy stood straight and said, "Make me!" He glared at both lawmen. "Which one of you is gonna go for his gun first?"

That was a question neither lawman knew the answer to. They were still trying to figure it out when Jimmy went out the door.

Johnny came out of the hotel, saw Clint Adams waiting for him in the empty street.

"I'm gonna kill you!" he swore.

"Bad move, Johnny," Clint said. "You'd do better to drop your gun in the street. Then I'll get Sheriff Cox and you can start back to New Mexico. Maybe they can't prove you did it. Maybe they'll have to let you go."

"I ain't goin' back," Johnny said. He dried his palms in his thighs. "I'm gonna kill you."

"Then come ahead, boy," Clint said. "I've got other things to do."

"I killed three men at one time," Johnny said. "They never cleared leather."

"They were probably all crippled."

"They was not!"

"Then come on. Step into the street. Let's see what you got . . . boy."

Johnny Creed licked his lips, stepped into the street.

FORTY-FOUR

When Jimmy Creed came out of the sheriff's office, he saw Clint Adams standing in the street. He stopped to see what was going on, saw Johnny come out of the hotel. He took a step, intending to run, then stopped. What if the kid could do it? What if he was faster than the Gunsmith? He figured the two of them together could take Clint Adams. He even figured he could do it alone, but what if the kid could do it? It would save him the trouble.

He started walking . . .

As Johnny stepped into the street, Clint started moving to his left. Johnny, in turn, moved right. Beyond Johnny, Clint could see Jimmy come running out of the sheriff's office and stop. The two lawmen had not been able to hold him back long enough, but it didn't look like the man was going to do anything. He was going to watch, and see if his son could do it.

"Johnny," Clint said, "your daddy's watching."

"You're lyin'."

"He's right behind you."

"You just want me to turn around so you can back-shoot me."

"No, not me. That's your father's rep."

"Never mind," Johnny said. "It don't even matter if he's watchin' or not."

"So you're really going to do this?"

"Stop talkin'!"

"Take your chances in New Mexico, Johnny," Clint said, "because you've got no chance here."

"Sonofa—" Johnny said, going for his gun.

The two lawmen came out of the office together, saw Jimmy Creed standing there. Down the street Clint Adams was in the street, facing Johnny Creed.

"They're gonna do it," Barrett said.

"Johnny'll kill 'im," Jimmy said. He looked over his shoulder at them. "You was tryin' to keep me busy, but I get to see this."

"Jimmy—" Cox said.

The sound of the shot cut him off.

Clint drew and fired. Johnny was fast. He got his hand on his gun before the bullet punched him in the chest. Clint thought about trying to shoot to wound, but he didn't know what Jimmy would be doing. And he couldn't take the chance that Johnny would still get a shot off. When a man drew his gun, he had to shoot to kill. It was the safest course of action.

Clint saw Johnny gasp, his eyes go wide in surprise,

and then he fell onto his face. He realized that he knew Johnny had killed Lanigan, but he couldn't prove it.

He holstered his gun, looked down the street, saw Jimmy Creed step down off the boardwalk.

"Jimmy—" Barrett said as Johnny fell.

"This is what you wanted, ain't it?" Jimmy asked. "To have us take care of each other? Then you don't have to do a thing."

"That's not—" Cox started, but Jimmy waved away their words and stepped into the street.

Clint watched Jimmy Creed approach. The man walked slowly, so Clint just stood there and waited. Finally, Jimmy reached the point where his son was lying facedown in the dirt.

"I told him not to do it, Jimmy," Clint said.

"Sure you did," Jimmy said. "You knew if you told him that, he'd do it."

"All he had to do was go back with Sheriff Cox," Clint said. "Maybe they wouldn't have been able to prove he killed the gambler."

"It don't matter," Jimmy said. "Don't matter now if he did it or not."

The two lawmen came walking down the street, stopped just far enough away to be able to hear the conversation.

"He did it, Jimmy," Clint said. "Didn't he tell you he did it? He just about said as much to me."

"Sure he did it," Jimmy said. "So what?"

Clint looked over at Cox, who nodded, indicating he'd heard the secondhand confession.

"So what now, Jimmy?" Clint asked. "You want to bury your son?"

"Naw," Jimmy said, "I wanna bury you, Adams."

"Not a good idea, Jimmy," Clint said. "You're not wanted in Arizona. Just bury your son and move on."

"Can't do that."

"Why? Because he was your son? When did you become a good father?"

"Naw, it ain't that," Jimmy said. "You're the Gunsmith. When will I get this chance again?"

"So it's all about reputation, huh?"

"How would you like to be known as a backshooter?" Jimmy asked. "This'll change that."

"Jimmy, you can't—"

Jimmy Creed went for his gun. Clint realized the father was not even as fast as the son had been. Clint had his gun out and had pulled the trigger before Jimmy could even touch his gun.

The elder Creed staggered back under the force of the bullet, fell into the street on his back, in the exact opposite pose as his dead son.

Clint ejected his spent shells and replaced them, walked over to the two fallen men, met the two lawmen there.

"You satisfied, Sheriff Cox?" he asked.

"I guess that's as close as I'll get to a confession," Cox said. "I'm satisfied."

"You satisfied, Adams?" Barrett asked.

"Me?" Clint asked. "No, Sheriff, I'm not satisfied at all. I never find killing a man satisfying. You got any objection to me leaving your town right now?"

"Naw," Sheriff Barrett said. "I don't have any objection to that at all."

Watch for

THE CLINT ADAMS SPECIAL

392nd novel in the exciting GUNSMITH series
from Jove

Coming in August!

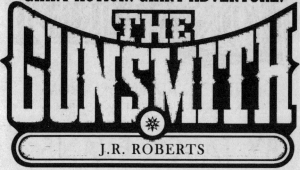

GIANT ACTION! GIANT ADVENTURE!

THE GUNSMITH

J.R. ROBERTS

penguin.com/actionwesterns

M455AS0812

GIANT-SIZED ADVENTURE FROM AVENGING ANGEL LONGARM.

BY TABOR EVANS

penguin.com/actionwesterns

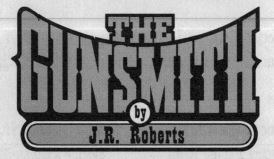